Deacon

The Carmichaels
Leigh Fenty

Chapter One

"You can go to jail for that, you know."

Deacon Carmichael watched his sister pace around the room. She was tall and slim, but full of piss and vinegar. They were a lot alike, which meant they often butted heads. But this was something he wasn't going to compromise on. She was making a mistake.

"Abigale, I'd sooner meet my maker than see you get involved with a cowboy. Especially a rodeo loving cowboy."

"That's pretty funny, considering you're a fourth-generation cowboy."

"That's exactly why I know what I'm talking about." Deacon sat on the edge of his desk. "Why do you have to be so difficult? I swear you're worse than your two brothers combined."

She folded her arms across her chest and glared at him. "I have three brothers, which is why you playing father doesn't work for me."

"I'm the closest thing you have to a father and have been since you were ten and still wearing braces." He shook his head. "God, I miss those days. Back when you looked up to me and listened to what I said."

"Back when you were my big brother and not my...keeper."

"Why get involved with someone now? You're headed to college in a few months."

She turned and headed for the door. "We'll see about that."

"Abby!" Deacon stood, then sat in the chair behind the desk. She'd begged him for a gap year between high school and college. One year turned into two and a half, but now it was time. She was going to college in January if he had to hogtie her and drag her there himself.

Tobias came through the door and glanced over his shoulder, then grinned at his older brother.

"What'd you say to her? She's pissed."

"When isn't she pissed?" Deacon picked up a cup of coffee and started to take a drink, before remembering it'd been sitting on his desk for over an hour. He looked at Tobias. "What do you want?"

"Wow. Love you too, brother." He dropped onto the couch. "I just wanted to tell you I'm in love."

"Again? What happened to the last one?"

Tobias waved at him. "False alarm. But this one. This one's the one." He put his boots up on the coffee table and crossed his ankles.

Deacon refrained from telling Tobias to get his feet off the table, and sighed. "I shouldn't ask, but which bar did you meet this one at?"

"Not a bar. Tanner's school."

Deacon cocked his head. "You can go to jail for that, you know."

Tobias laughed. "She's not a student. She's a teacher. Just started last week. English I think. Or maybe math." He shrugged. "Doesn't really matter."

Deacon knew exactly who his brother was talking about. "Tall brunette. Slim. Hazel eyes?"

Tobias put his feet on the floor and leaned forward. "You know her?"

"Sure. She introduced herself to me when I picked Tanner up the other day."

"You've met her?"

"You haven't?"

"Not yet."

Deacon laughed. "Then how do you know she's the one?"

Tobias leaned back again. "I feel it in my heart, man."

"Yeah. I know where you're feeling it. It isn't in your heart."

"What's her name?"

"Um..." Deacon shook his head. "Can't recall."

Tobias got to his feet. "You're not interested in her, are you?"

Deacon shook his head. "If I was, I'd probably remember her name. She's all yours. Been there, done that. I don't have the time or patience to get tangled up with another woman. You might want to actually talk to her, though. I believe she mentioned a boyfriend."

Tobias shrugged. "Minor inconvenience." He headed for the door. "You should really lay off Abby, she's damn near a woman."

"She's twenty."

"I'm pretty sure Mother had you when she was nineteen."

"That's different."

Tobias stopped at the door and looked at Deacon. "How so? She was married to a rodeo loving cowboy."

"Butch Kiefer isn't Dad."

"I'm pretty sure at the time Grandpa had the same reservations as you. But you're right. Abby can do better than Butch." He went out the door.

Deacon called after him. "Will you tell her that, please?"

He stood and went to the bar in the corner of the room. It was more of a high narrow table with a selection of alcohol, some glasses, and an ice bucket. But his father had always called it a bar, so the name stuck.

The office was exactly like Clint left it the day he died, right down to the table Tobias just had his boots on. The mantle over the brick fireplace had family pictures on it that hadn't been updated in ten years. And the big desk Deacon spent too much time at, was the same desk he and Tobias had used as a fort when they were boys.

Deacon lifted the lid on the ice bucket and found it empty. "Straight scotch it is." He poured himself a healthy shot, then returned to the desk. That was one thing he had changed. His father drank bourbon. Deacon like scotch.

He took a drink and leaned back in his chair. Abby was right. He was her older brother, not her father. But when Clint Carmichael died ten years ago, leaving a shattered wife and four children, someone had to take over. That someone was Deacon. So at the age of twenty-three, he became the head of the family, which included running the two-hundred-thousand acre Starlight Ranch.

At the time, Tobias was in high school, and Abby and Tanner were in elementary school. Clint, still a young man at forty-eight, fell off a horse, cracked his skull, and died three days later, having never regained consciousness. His devastated wife, Faith, fell into a two year depression, leaving Deacon to keep the family and the ranch together.

He took a sip of scotch. He didn't use to drink at four in the afternoon, but lately, it seemed he needed it to get through the rest of the night. A scotch before dinner, a brandy after dinner. And another scotch before bed. He really didn't feel that was excessive.

Tonight, he might need a bit more. It was September fifteenth. The night of the annual Starlight Gala, followed by formal horsemanship games tomorrow, an auction, a barbecue, and a less formal barn dance. On Sunday was the rodeo, a chili cook-off, and a lot of drinking in the beer tent. It was a long weekend of being social with fellow ranchers, horse buyers from around the country, and the local cowboys. It was the end of the long working summer and the beginning of a series of social events continuing until New Year's Eve. And to Deacon, it was all a nightmare.

————————◦❦◦————————

Dinner was served promptly at six, and Faith expected all of her children to be there on time. In her mind, it seemed to justify her otherwise mostly non-existent presence in their everyday lives. When her husband died, Faith's spirit went with him. But at dinner, she was the family matriarch. So when Deacon came in five minutes late, she gave him a look that made him feel like he was a child again.

"Sorry, Mother." He sat next to his youngest brother, Tanner, and across from Abby and Tobias. Faith sat at the end of the table. The opposite end had a place setting and an empty chair. Ten years after his death, Clint Carmichael still had a place at the dinner table.

Faith said grace. Then the plates of roast beef, potatoes, and green beans were passed around the table. The food at the Carmichael dinner table was usually simple, but always good. Their cook, Ruthie, who also served as housekeeper had been with the family since before Deacon was born. When Faith dropped out after Clint's death. Ruthie also took on the role of nanny to Tanner and Abby.

Tanner was visibly excited as he gulped his food down.

Faith looked at him. "Tanner, if you don't slow down, you're going to choke."

"Yes, ma'am." He swallowed hard and took a sip of iced tea.

Tobias laughed. "Yeah. You don't want to die before you make it to your first gala."

Faith frowned, and he said, "Sorry, Mother."

Abby pushed some green beans around her plate. "I heard the Wexler sisters are going to be there."

Tobias glanced at Tanner. "Who are the Wexler sisters?"

Abby ate a single green bean. "Tanner is sweet on one of them."

"I am not."

Tobias grinned. "Which one?"

Abby shrugged. "I don't know. I can't tell them apart."

Tanner sighed. "Hallie is much more... Well, she's... They're not the same."

Tobias shook his head. "What am I missing?"

Abby leaned toward Tanner. "They're identical twins. Of course, they're the same."

Tobias leaned back in his chair. "I was in love with a twin once. Tanner's right. Once you get to know them, they're not the same."

Deacon cleared his throat. "If I recall, you dated both of the Sinclair twins."

Tobias laughed. "Yeah. But one at a time."

Faith set her fork down. "Are all my children going to the gala alone this year?"

Everyone nodded but Abby.

Deacon looked at her. "Please don't tell me you're going with Butch."

"He might be there."

"I'm pretty sure he isn't on the guest list."

"I invited him. I'm a Carmichael. I can invite who I want."

"That's not how it works. Like it or not. Fair or not. There's a pecking order. And the gala is for those at the top of it. The cowboys have their own dance tomorrow night."

Faith took a roll and buttered it. "If your young man shows up, we certainly won't turn him away. But you should've asked Deacon or me about it."

"It's so elitist."

Deacon took a sip of his tea. "It's the way it has been for over a hundred years. You can't fight tradition."

"Well, then, maybe I won't go in protest to your snobbery."

Faith smiled at Abby. "Of course you'll go."

Abby glanced at Deacon, then looked at Faith. "Yes, Mother."

Faith looked at her middle son. "I expect you to behave tonight, Tobias."

He grinned at her. "Of course. I always behave."

She pointed a finger at him. "No mischief."

"I would never."

Deacon kicked him under the table. "I'll keep an eye on him, Mother."

"You shouldn't need to babysit your twenty-six-year-old brother. You need to enjoy yourself and take advantage of the many single women attending tonight."

"I'd rather babysit."

Deacon and Tobias both went for the last piece of roast at the same time, with Tobias' fork landing an instant before Deacon's.

Tobias grinned as he dropped the slice of meat onto his plate. "Your oldest son has sworn off women, Mother. He says, and this is a direct quote, 'I don't have the time or patience to get tangled up with another woman.'"

"Nonsense. It's time you settle down and start a family of your own."

Deacon pushed his empty plate aside and wiped his mouth with a napkin. "And when would I find the time to do that?"

Abby pushed her chair back and stood. "You could stop running my life. That'd free up some time for you."

Faith looked at her. "And where are you off to? We haven't had dessert yet."

"I need to get ready for the gala, Mother. So you can show me off to all your friend's eligible sons."

Tobias laughed. "Probably should've started a little earlier."

Abby slapped the back of his head. "Shut up." She marched off.

Faith shook her head. "Abigale!" When Abby didn't stop, Faith looked at Tobias. "I told you to behave."

"You said to behave at the gala."

Tanner stood. "May I be excused? I want to go get ready too."

"Of course, darling."

Deacon watched Tanner leave the room. "Was I that excited to go to my first gala?"

Before she could answer, Tobias interrupted. "You've never been excited about anything in your life."

"I was pretty damn excited the day you left for college."

Tobias threw his napkin at Deacon and Faith got to her feet.

"Boys, enough. And Deacon, no swearing at the table."

Tobias laughed. "Yeah, big brother, watch your damn mouth."

"Both of you, go get dressed. Dinner's over."

Tobias frowned. "What about dessert?"

"There will be plenty of sweet treats at the gala."

Tobias nudged Deacon as they left the room. "I'm counting on it. Did you invite the school teacher?"

"Why would I invite the school teacher?"

"Abby's right, you are a snob."

Chapter Two

"We can't go as the Carmichael twins!"

Abby studied her reflection in the full-length mirror. It wasn't the dress she wanted. This one her mother picked out was much more conservative than the dress she wanted.

"I'm twenty years old and my mother is still dressing me." She tilted her head. It wasn't a bad dress. The emerald green complimented her dark hair and gray eyes. And the neckline, while not as low as she'd like, it was flattering. "Fine. Mother was right again."

As she began fixing her hair, her phone rang. She knew the ringtone. It was Butch.

She picked up the phone. "Hey."

"Hi, Abby."

"You're coming tonight, right?"

"Um...no."

Abby sat on the edge of her bed. "Why not?"

"Because. Well, I was talking to the guys, and it wouldn't be right."

"What do you mean?"

"The gala is for the bigwigs. I wouldn't be welcome."

She picked up the one stuffed animal she still had on her bed. It was a horse Deacon had gotten her the first Christmas after their father died. "You'd be coming as my guest."

"That doesn't matter. I like you and all. I'd do most anything for you. But it'd be like betraying my buddies."

"Wow."

"I'm sorry. But tomorrow night at the barn dance, I'm all yours."

She set the horse aside and got to her feet. "So, I can come to your dance, but you can't come to mine?"

"It's okay for you to slum. But it's not okay for me to pretend I'm something I'm not."

"Fine. Whatever."

"So, I'll see you tomorrow night?"

"If I feel like slumming it with the lowly cowboys, I might drop by."

"Abby, come on."

"I've got a gala to get ready for." She ended the call and tossed her phone on the bedside table.

She enjoyed some of the perks of being a member of the Carmichael family. But mostly she hated it.

When Faith knocked on the door, then opened it and peeked in, Abby smiled at her.

"You look beautiful, Mother." A couple times a year, Faith Carmichael became a semblance of the woman she once was. The gala was one of those times. She'd been hosting it for years. And to everyone who saw her there, they'd never suspect it was a well-rehearsed persona that didn't reflect who she'd become.

"As do you. That dress is perfect."

Abby turned back to the mirror. "I have to admit, it's a pretty great dress."

Faith came up behind her and ran her fingers through Abby's long hair. "And what are you going to do with this?"

"I'd like to wear it down. But I might get too hot."

Faith separated sections from both sides of Abby's head. "How about a compromise? Off your face, but down in the back."

Abby sighed. "You're right again, Mother."

"What's wrong?"

Abby sat on the bed. "He's not coming."

"It's probably for the best, dear."

"Dad was a cowboy when you met him, right?"

"Yes. He rode broncs. But he was also a Carmichael."

"So because Butch doesn't come from one of the Texas ten, he's not as good?"

"Of course not, Abby. But because you're a Carmichael, and our family owns the second largest ranch in the Texas panhandle, we need to adhere to certain standards. You can have fun with your cowboy, but when it comes time to get serious about a young man, he needs to come from the right family."

"That is so...nineteenth century. Your family isn't nearly as wealthy as ours. Why was it okay for father to marry...below his station?" When Faith didn't answer her, Abby backtracked. "I'm sorry, Mother. I didn't mean you weren't worthy or anything."

"I know dear. By Carmichael standards, I certainly wasn't who your grandparents had in mind for their only son. But your father wasn't going to be stopped from marrying for love."

"That's so romantic."

"That was your father." Faith kissed her on the forehead. "I know it seems old fashioned. And it is changing. I want you to be happy. And I want you to find someone you love. But I don't imagine that person is Butch Kiefer. There are plenty of men to choose from that can afford to give you the life you deserve." She held out her hand. "Come, let me fix your hair."

"Well, if it's one of the rich spoiled boys I've spent twelve years in private school with, then I'm not so sure I'll find my Prince Charming amongst them."

Deacon was tying his tie when Tanner came into his room and Deacon looked at his brother through the mirror. "What's up, kid?"

"My tie. I've been trying for twenty minutes."

Deacon smiled and turned to him, then tied the tie. He took a step back. "There you go."

Tanner was shorter than him and Tobias. He took after their mother, blond, blue eyes, and shorter than the Carmichael side of the family. Deacon and Tobias were six-one and six-two respectively, while Tanner stopped growing at five-ten. The two older brothers, along with Abby, had their father's coloring. Abby was tall as well, being only an inch shorter than Tanner. The young man was relieved when he passed her up at age sixteen.

Deacon watched Tanner fiddle with his tie. "So, who's this girl Abby was teasing you about?"

"Hallie Wexler."

"The Double R?"

"Yeah."

"They RSVPed."

"Yeah. But her dad will be there. He's a real…hard ass."

Deacon laughed. "And you're a Carmichael. I doubt he'll have a problem with his daughter dancing with you."

"Dancing. Maybe. Dating. I'm not so sure."

"Well, start with the dancing and see where it leads."

"Thanks, Deacon." He headed for the door, then stopped and turned back. "Why don't you like the gala?"

"It's not that I don't like it. It serves its purpose, which is rubbing shoulders with the right people, and flirting with the right women. But I'm not interested in finding the right woman. And I rub shoulders with most of these people throughout the year. It seems pointless. And a waste of my time."

"You don't think it's just a show of money and power?"

"Oh, no. I do. But it's part of what makes our world go round."

Tanner shrugged, before turning toward the door once more.

"Hey kid, steer clear of the punch."

"I know. I was with Tobias when he bought the rum."

Deacon laughed, took one last look in the mirror, then followed Tanner into the hall.

The Carmichael home was a massive and rambling two-story house. The four bedrooms upstairs were the size of small apartments, with their own bath and a sitting area. At thirty-three, Deacon sometimes felt like he shouldn't still be living in his mother's house. But his office was here. And she expected him to be at dinner every night unless he was out of town. So it was convenient. He also needed to be available for her when she spiraled, which was happening more and more often. She needed him when she was at her lowest. He was the only one who could comfort her.

Downstairs was an expansive living room, a den which housed a large collection of books, a pool table, and an actual stocked bar with a mini fridge and a sink. There was a formal dining room, used for guests, and the family dining room where they ate most of their meals. The large kitchen also contained a table and a breakfast bar. Deacon's office was on one side of the living room, and Faith's suite was off the other. Next to that were two guest rooms. But the Carmichaels hadn't hosted any guests in quite some time.

Most of the other ranches had bigger and fancier houses, but the Carmichael house was built by Deacon's great-grandfather and no one in the family ever wanted anything else. So, other than a few electrical and plumbing upgrades, the house remained the same.

The house would someday be his, but he had forty acres picked out on a ridge overlooking the pastures and far enough away from the main house to give him some privacy. He'd build a house there someday. But for now, convenience outweighed his need for privacy.

Deacon knocked on Tobias' door. "Time to go."

Tobias opened the door, then frowned at Deacon's dark blue suit. "I thought you were wearing your gray pinstripe."

"I changed my mind."

Tobias glanced at his own dark blue suit. "We can't go as the Carmichael twins!"

Tanner laughed. "You guys do look an awful lot alike."

Deacon shook his head. "No one's going to care."

"Just give me five. I'll be right down."

Deacon continued down the hall to Abby's door while Tanner ran ahead and took the stairs two at a time.

"Abigale, you ready?"

He waited a moment before she opened the door. "Yeah. I'm coming."

"Beautiful dress."

"Of course you like it."

"What does that mean?"

"Mother chose it. Or shall I say, encouraged me to get it."

"Mother has good taste. She's been doing this for about thirty-six years. She knows what she's talking about."

Abby wrapped a shawl around her shoulders. "Whatever." She went into the hall, then looked behind them. "Where's Tobias?"

"He's coming."

She looked at his suit. "I thought you were wearing your gray pinstripe."

"I changed my mind."

"So I have to wear what Mother tells me to, but you get to wear what you want?"

"Thirteen years."

"What?"

"In thirteen years, you can wear whatever the hell you want."

They went down the stairs and found Tanner and Faith waiting by the door.

Faith looked at the stairs. "Where's your brother?"

Deacon stopped next to her. "He's coming."

She ran a hand down the front of his suit jacket. "You look just like your father in this suit."

Before Deacon could respond, Tobias jogged down the stairs in a dark gray suit. He stopped at the bottom, held his arms out, and spun around.

"Perfect, right?"

Deacon adjusted his tie. "Next to me and Tanner, you'll be the third best looking Carmichael at the gala."

Abby slapped his arm. "Hey."

"Oh, sorry, Abigale. Make that fourth."

She smiled. "Thank you."

They left the house and got into the Escalade. Deacon didn't like to be driven anywhere, but on Gala night, Faith insisted they have a driver. So he helped her into the passenger seat, then got in the backseat next to Tobias. Tanner and Abby got into the third seat.

They drove ten miles to the Connelly house. It was the home of the first mayor of the town of Connelly and its namesake. The home had been a museum for fifty years. The gala was held in the large main room and spilled out into the extensive gardens.

The driver pulled up to the grand entrance and Deacon helped his mother out of the car. The Carmichaels had hosted the gala for the last thirty-five years. Faith took over twenty years ago when her mother-in-law passed the torch to her. Someday, it'd be the job of Deacon's wife, assuming he ever decided to marry.

Faith entered the room and immediately became the center of attention. Deacon bowed out of the spotlight and made the rounds, making sure everything was in order. He had to stop several times to make polite conversation. He hated polite conversation. He hated pompous affairs. But this was his life. With his father gone, he was the de facto host alongside his mother.

When Tanner came up to him looking giddy and preoccupied, Deacon pulled him aside.

"What's got you all wired up?"

"She's here."

"Hallie Wexler?"

"Yeah. And Hester. And their parents. I think she smiled at me, but I'm not sure."

"If she caught sight of you, I'm sure she smiled." Deacon adjusted Tanner's tie. "You're quite worthy of dating a Wexler sister."

"Thanks. She looks really pretty."

"I'm sure she does."

"When should I ask her to dance?"

"Give it a little bit. You don't want to seem too anxious."

"Right. I need to be cool." He took a deep breath and blew it out slowly.

Deacon squeezed Tanner's shoulder as he looked at the Wexler twins across the room. "So, which one is Hallie?"

"The one in the blue dress."

"Ah. Yes. She's quite beautiful. Go outside and get some air, then go ask her to dance."

"What if she says no?"

"You give it an hour and then you go ask her again."

Chapter Three

"Mmm. That gets the blood flowing."

The gala was in full swing and Deacon was trying to keep busy, making sure everything was running smoothly. Faith didn't need him overseeing things. She had people to do that for her. But it gave him something to do and kept the women at bay. It wasn't a matter of conceit. He was a Carmichael. The oldest son. He'd be a catch for any of the young single women attending tonight. But Deacon didn't want to get caught. Like he told Tobias. "Been there. Done that." He had one serious relationships, and it turned out the woman was more interested in his money than in him. Besides, like he'd said at dinner, he didn't have the time.

When he wandered by the table with an enormous crystal punch bowl and matching crystal cups, he frowned at the young man behind the table.

"Why is the bowl half-empty?"

"Um... I was about to refill it, sir."

"Don't wait until it's almost empty. Keep it topped off. It's your only job, right?"

The young man nodded. "Yes, sir. And filling cups."

"Well, you can't fill cups from an empty punch bowl."

"Yes, sir. I'll do it now."

"Thank you." Deacon turned away from the table and ran into a tall, slim brunette with hazel eyes. "Oh, sorry." He looked at her, then pointed. "School teacher."

She gave him a curt smile and pointed at him. "Asshole."

"Excuse me?" He laughed. "Did you just call me an asshole?"

"Yes. I did."

"Why?"

"Did you not just berate that poor young man because the punch bowl was down a few inches?"

"Yes. I believe that was me." She looked quite different than she had at school. She was dressed in a light yellow gown that was simple, but quite attractive on her. Her makeup highlighted her hazel eyes, and her hair was in a loose bun with tiny flowers tucked in here and there.

She stepped by him and picked up a pre-filled cup. "Is it good?"

"It'll be better in a while after my brother spikes it."

"Your brother?"

"Tobias. Who happens to be in love with you, by the way."

"Seeing as I don't know Tobias, I find that highly unlikely."

"True none the less. But don't worry. He'll get over it. He falls in love on a regular basis. It rarely sticks."

"How lucky for me?"

The young man returned and filled the bowl from a pitcher.

Deacon glanced at him and mumbled. "Thank you," then turned back to the woman. "You introduced yourself last week, but I can't quite remember your name."

"Cassidy O'Hare."

He shook her offered hand. "Deacon Carmichael."

"Of course. I should've known."

He didn't ask her what she meant by that. "You're here with Winston O'Hare?"

"My grandfather. Did you think I crashed your party?"

"I wasn't sure. You wouldn't be the first. And I doubt anyone would've questioned your right to be here." He loved how she wasn't the least bit intimidated by him.

She took a sip of punch and wrinkled her nose, then set her cup on the tray meant for used ones. "To be honest with you, which I always am, I only came to observe the archaic elitism of your yearly event. The class distinction in northwestern Texas astounds me."

Deacon smiled. "You should meet my sister. You two would get along great. And as one of the archaic entitled snobs, I'll tell you a secret. I agree with you." He acquired a Texas drawl. "But here on the Texas panhandle, that's the way things are, and have been since the first settlers arrived to build the foundations of what you see now." He pointed a finger at her. "And it seems to me, you're overlooking the fact that your grandfather is a member of this exclusive club of rich ranchers."

"My grandfather is nothing like you."

"You don't know me."

"I know enough. I know what people say about you."

"And what's that?"

She took a moment to answer. "That you're driven. A workaholic. That since you've been in charge you've tripled the value of your ranch."

"Did they also say, I work right beside my men? That I thank God everyday for allowing me to live in this beautiful country? And that I know everything my family has is due to the men that have come before us? Don't judge a book by the company he keeps, Miss. O'Hare."

She frowned at him. "You're mixing metaphors."

"I know, English teacher. I went to college."

She folded her arms across her chest. "So if you're such a man of the people, why don't you change things? It seems someone in your position could affect change."

"I don't know where you've been for the last..." He studied her for a moment to assess her age. "For the last twenty-fivish years. But you can't buck tradition. It is what it is."

"That's a cop out, Mr. Carmichael." She turned and walked away from him.

He watched her go. "Good luck with that one, Tobias."

As Deacon wandered away in the opposite direction, Tobias came up and took his arm. "That was her. You were just talking to the school teacher." He raised up on his toes to watch her across the room. "You said she wasn't invited."

"Turns out, she's Winston O'Hare's granddaughter."

"The hell you say."

"That's what she said."

"That's fantastic news."

"How so?"

"She's one of us."

Deacon smiled and put a hand on Tobias' shoulder. "I'm afraid Miss O'Hare is very far from being one of us."

"What's her first name? I'm going to ask her to dance." He patted his jacket pocket. "As soon as I take care of the punch."

"Cassidy."

"I love it. Do you want to help with the ah...?"

"Sure. Why not?"

"You distract the kid. I'll take care of the rest."

They approached the table and the young man came to attention. "The bowl is full, sir."

Deacon picked up the tray of used glasses. "Do you really think our guests want to look at dirty cups?"

"No, sir. Of course not." He took the tray from Deacon and headed for the kitchen. Deacon nodded to Tobias. "I'll leave you to it. I know nothing." He walked away as Tobias pulled the bottle from his pocket and emptied it into the punch.

———————⚜———————

Cassidy was watching the party from the sidelines. Her grandfather had wandered off, leaving her in a room full of people she didn't know. When a tall, dark-haired man approached her, the family resemblance was obvious. It had to be the second son of the Carmichael family. She thought about what Deacon had said. Was this man with the beautiful smile truly in love with her? Of course not. But she was curious, just the same.

He came right up to her and gave her a slight nod. "Cassidy O'Hare?"

"That's correct."

"I believe you are my little brother's math teacher."

"English."

"Even better."

"Why is that better?"

"Because I didn't flunk English." He offered his hand. "Tobias Carmichael."

She put her hand in his. "Nice to meet you." When he held onto her hand longer than he should've, she gently retrieved it. "I was just talking to your brother."

"Oh, sorry."

She smiled. "Why sorry?"

"He's not much fun."

"And you are?"

"Oh, yeah. I'm extremely fun. Would you care to have some punch with me?"

"I tried the punch. It's not very good."

He took her arm. "Trust me. It's much better, now."

They began walking toward the punch bowl. "So, this *better* punch. Aren't you the least bit concerned that some of the younger people, or even older people, might not want to drink it?"

He patted her hand. "It's tradition. Everyone knows it's...*better*. If they don't want to partake, they drink lemonade. My brother and his friends prefer soft drinks. So, it's all good."

"So before you were old enough to make the punch...*better*. Who did it?"

"That would be Deacon."

Cassidy stopped walking. "That seems highly out of character."

"Now, maybe. But back in the day, he was actually sort of fun."

"What happened to him?"

He took a moment. "Our father died."

"Oh, I'm so sorry." Her grandfather had told her Deacon was the head of the family. But he didn't say how that came about.

Tobias shrugged as they arrived at the punch bowl. He smiled at the server. "Two please."

"Yes, sir, Mr. Carmichael."

They were each handed a crystal cup, and Tobias tapped Cassidy's, then leaned in close. "It becomes weaker as the night goes on. This is as good as it gets."

Cassidy took a sip. "Oh. My goodness." She blew out a breath. "I'm not sure I'd use the word good to describe it." It tasted a lot like paint thinner. Not that she was in the habit of drinking paint thinner. "What did you put in here? Rum?"

"It's the only thing worth drinking." Tobias drank his in one gulp. "Mmm. That gets the blood flowing."

Cassidy raised an eyebrow, then drank the rest of her punch. She covered her mouth as her eyes watered. "Wow. I see what you mean." She held back a cough.

Tobias seemed impressed, and he grinned. "Would you care to dance, Cassidy?"

The man was charming. And while the love at first sight thing was odd, she was intrigued. "Sure. Why not?"

The music was provided by a twelve-piece orchestra, playing songs from the big band era.

Tobias pulled Cassidy in close. "Every year I try to convince my mother to hire a band who plays something a little more modern. Even stuff from the fifties and sixties would be better than this. The Beatles, Elton John. Hell, even Barry Manilow would be better than this."

"I kind of like it."

"So, why don't I remember you growing up around here?"

"Because I didn't. But I spent most summers here until I graduated from high school."

"You did?"

"Yes. And I remember watching you and Deacon compete in the Texas version of showjumping."

"Oh, yeah. Deacon still competes once in a while. He'll be riding tomorrow, actually."

"Not you?"

"No. I fell and broke my leg a few years ago. It left me unable to control the horse correctly for competition."

"Deacon's riding tomorrow?"

"Yeah. But we're both chasing the hounds tomorrow morning."

"Chasing the hounds?"

"Another event we borrowed from the English. Only we do it, Texas style."

Cassidy leaned back and looked at him. "Please don't tell me you set the dogs on a poor fox."

"Oh no. We send a few riders out with a scent, then once they have a good lead, we set the hounds loose. The riders follow the hounds. It's more of a race, actually. The first rider to cross the finish line, wins. For the last five years, it's been the Carmichaels."

"You've won five years in a row?"

"We're the Carmichaels."

"Why should that matter?"

"It shouldn't. But it does." He shrugged. "I've learned to live with it."

"You live in a very interesting world, Tobias." They continued dancing. "And where's the finish line?"

Tobias shrugged. "Only the scent riders know. It's usually about twenty miles of cross-country riding."

"Sounds dangerous."

"Not at all. It's a blast. Anyone can join. Do you ride?"

She settled into his arms again. "I ride a little."

"I hope to see you there in the morning, then. Bright and early. You can be on our team."

"Who else is on the team?"

"Just me and Deacon so far."

"How early is bright and early?"

"Eight o'clock. Followed by a pancake breakfast on the front lawn."

They danced in silence for a few moments, then Tobias leaned back and looked at her.

"So, I heard a nasty rumor about you having a boyfriend."

"Would that be a problem?"

"I'm not too worried. I like to be challenged. But is it true?"

She shook her head. "Not anymore."

He nodded. "Good to know."

Abby spent the evening talking with some of the girls, most of whom she didn't like very much. And she danced several times with boys she'd known most of her life. They all went to the same private school and attended the same parties every year. It was all boring and the reason why she was so interested in Butch Kiefer. She wasn't particularly attracted to him, but he wasn't one of the inner circle and that seemed adventurous and a bit dangerous.

When she spotted her mother heading her way with a blond man she couldn't quite place, she steeled herself for an introduction. She wasn't sure who he was, but if Mother was bringing him to her, he was considered worthy of spending time with a Carmichael.

Faith took Abby's hand. "Abigale, dear, you remember Skyler Fremont. He's back from Harvard.

Abby did remember Skyler. He was two years ahead of her in school. She just didn't remember him looking so good. Not only was he at least six feet, his bright blue eyes and blond hair were perfect. He'd definitely grown into a man during his four years at Harvard. He was also from the biggest ranch in northwestern Texas, making him an even better catch than her brothers. Not that that interested her. She could care less how much money his family had.

He smiled and offered his hand. "Abby."

"Skyler. Of course I remember you."

He shook her hand. "I don't suppose you'd—"

"I'd love to."

Skyler took her arm and led her to the dance floor. Once there, he lost the polite smile. "Let's get this over with."

"Excuse me?"

"I've been watching you all night. You're as bored as I am."

She studied him for a moment. "You've been watching me?"

"Well, you know. Not constantly."

They started dancing. "So, I take it you hate the gala as much as I do?"

"It's so...elitist."

Abby smiled. "I totally agree."

Chapter Four

"Everyone has a role to play."

Deacon had run out of things to oversee and was now standing in a corner, trying to be invisible. He'd danced a few times because he couldn't talk his way out of it. When he spotted Cassidy headed his way, he gave her a nod and a quick smile.

"Cassidy."

"Your remembered my name, this time."

"I'll never forget it again. I hope you're enjoying yourself."

"I suppose since you're the host, I should say yes. But, honestly, this isn't really my thing."

"What is your thing?"

She shrugged. "Anything but this."

When he noticed a woman headed toward him, who'd been after him all night to dance, he took Cassidy's arm. "I don't suppose you'd like to dance and save me from Bess Brighton?"

"The North Fork Ranch?"

He smiled. "You know your ranch families?" He started leading her to the dance floor.

"My grandfather gave me a cheat sheet." She looked at him. "I don't remember actually agreeing to dance with you."

"Are you really going to leave me standing here?"

"That would be kind of embarrassing, I guess."

He took her in his arms. "This is strictly a rescue mission."

"Oh, that's flattering."

Deacon laughed. "Well, since my brother is in love with you, anything else would be highly inappropriate."

"Right. Of course." They danced for a few moments. "So, do I not have a say in this whole Tobias is in love with me thing?"

"He'll get over it. He always does. But until then, I'm afraid you're stuck." She felt good in his arms. But he tried not to think about it. She smelled good too. Like roses. But very subtle.

"I don't even remember meeting him before tonight."

"Yeah. You didn't. He saw you when he picked up Tanner today."

She looked at him. "Today? He fell in love with me today?"

"Yes."

"Must be serious."

Deacon laughed. "Where did you live before you came here to teach my brother English?"

"Austin."

"But you spent summers here with your grandfather. I remember you."

"I doubt that."

"No. Really. Braids, braces, a pink cowboy hat."

"That could describe most any pre-teen visiting her grandfather's ranch."

"You had a horse named…Bumble Bee."

She pulled back and looked at him. "Why would you remember that?"

"I'm not so good with people. But I remember horses."

Tobias was watching Deacon and Cassidy dancing when Faith came up to him.

"Why aren't you out there having fun?"

He glanced at her. "My brother is dancing with the schoolteacher."

Faith looked at Deacon and Cassidy across the room on the dance floor. "School teacher?"

"Winston O'Hare's granddaughter and Tanner's English teacher.

"She's very lovely. She looks like her mother."

"You knew her mother?"

"Yes. Her father, Winston Jr., left the ranch to marry her. It was quite the scandal. She was an artist and a free spirit. She hated the whole ranch life. Broke poor Winston's heart. Junior was his only child." She leaned in close. "Word is, he's planning on leaving everything to his granddaughter."

"How do you know all this?"

She patted his arm. "Everyone knows."

"Do you suppose that's why she's here?"

Faith shrugged. "I don't know."

He grinned. "I'm going to go cut in on my brother."

"Since when do you care whether someone has money or not?"

"I don't. I fell in love with her when I thought she was just a school teacher."

"And when was that?"

"This afternoon."

Tobias left Faith and crossed the dance floor to get to Deacon and Cassidy. He tapped Deacon on the shoulder.

"I'm pretty sure there's some waiter somewhere that needs to be yelled at."

Deacon cocked his head at Tobias, then nodded to Cassidy. "Thank you for the rescue."

He walked away, and Tobias took Cassidy's hand. "Sorry. That must've been terribly boring for you." They started dancing.

Cassidy pulled back from his grip, which was a little too close. "So, Deacon tells me you're in love with me."

"He shouldn't have. I wanted to tell you myself."

"You know it's impossible, right?"

He pulled her in close again. "Shhh. Don't ruin this moment."

"We're having a moment?"

"I don't know about you. But I definitely am."

They continued dancing without further conversation. When the music stopped, Cassidy stepped away from Tobias.

"I need to go check in with my grandfather."

"I'll go with you. I haven't said hi to him yet."

Cassidy sighed. "You're a bit like a piece of gum on the bottom of my shoe."

Tobias laughed. "Stuck on you?"

"I was thinking more along the lines of an annoyance."

He took her arm. "You just need to get to know me."

"It doesn't seem I'm going to have much of a choice in the matter."

He grinned. "You're funny. And feisty. I like that."

They approached Winston, and Cassidy kissed him on the cheek. "Granddad."

"My dear. Are you allowing yourself to have some fun?"

She glanced at Tobias. "Yes."

Tobias offered his hand to Winston. "Good evening, sir."

"Tobias. I hope you're behaving yourself this evening."

"Always, sir."

Winston raised an eyebrow. "I've had the punch."

Tobias smiled. "It was a very expensive bottle of rum."

"I noticed. If nothing else, you know your alcohol."

Tobias bowed slightly. "From one connoisseur to another." He smiled at Cassidy. "I'm going to go track down my sister. I saw her hanging out with Skyler Fremont, which can only lead to trouble."

Deacon was cornered by three women when he spotted his mother approaching. He smiled at the women. "Sorry, ladies, I believe my mother is looking for me."

He slipped away and went to Faith.

She smiled. "I didn't mean to interrupt."

He took her arm. "Always interrupt when you see me surrounded by the enemy."

"My darling boy, how am I ever going to get you married off?"

"You're not."

"We'll see about that. Have you seen your brother?"

"Which one?" She looked at him, and he added, "Oh, right. No, not since he cut in on my dance with Cassidy O'Hare."

"Lovely girl."

"Hmm. I hadn't noticed."

Faith patted his hand. "Go find him. And check on Abby, too. Seems young Skyler has latched onto her."

"Really. He seems like perfect son-in-law material."

"The boy doesn't necessarily reflect his family's views."

"Do you think she's found a comrade in him?"

"Just go see what she's up to."

Deacon kissed her cheek. "I'll go rein in the two troublesome Carmichaels."

After twenty minutes of searching, he found Tobias in one of the closed rooms. He was sitting on a red velvet couch with his foot resting on a table. He had a bottle of rum in his hand, which he held up when he spotted Deacon.

"You found me."

Deacon looked around the room right out of the Victorian age. "I'm pretty sure this room is off-limits. Even for a Carmichael."

"Come have a drink with me, brother."

"Where did you get the bottle?"

"I brought a spare for the punch. But then I figured, why waste it on all those people out there?" He took a drink.

"Is your leg bothering you?"

"No more than usual." He took another drink.

"Maybe you should hold off a little on the rum. I don't need my partner for the race in the morning, hungover."

"You know I ride the same, sober, drunk, or hungover. Badly. I ride badly no matter what my condition is."

"Let me take you home."

Tobias put his leg on the floor with a wince, then looked at Deacon. "Do you like Cassidy?"

Deacon shook his head. "I meant what I said about being out of the game."

Tobias pointed at him. "That doesn't answer the question."

"I've no interest in Cassidy. And even if I did. I wouldn't act upon it until you moved on to the next love of your life."

"You think I'm flighty. And maybe I have been in the past. But Cassidy..." He smiled. "There's something about her."

Deacon walked to him and took the bottle out of his hand. "Well, let's not let her meet Prince Charming's drunken twin."

"Prince not Charming?"

"Yeah. That's the one."

"Help me up."

Deacon helped Tobias to his feet. "We'll go through the garden."

"Right. To keep the disappointing Carmichael out of sight."

"You're not a disappointment. You've just had too much to drink."

Tobias patted Deacon's chest. "You're wrong. I haven't had too much to drink yet. I can still see straight, and the fire in my leg is still burning."

They went through a back entrance that took them to the garden. There were several people enjoying the cool night air, but they were too engrossed in their conversations to pay the Carmichael brothers much attention.

When Deacon spotted Abby and Skyler, he steered Tobias to a bench. "Sit tight for a minute."

Tobias took the bottle of rum out of Deacon's pocket. "Take your time."

Deacon retrieved the bottle. "I'll be right back."

He tucked the bottle into his pocket and crossed the garden to Abby and Skyler, who didn't see him approaching.

When Skyler handed Abby a cup of punch, he heard him say, "One drink won't kill you."

Deacon stepped up and took the cup from Abby. "No. But it might kill *you*."

Skyler took a step back. "Deacon."

"Skyler."

Abby scowled at Deacon. "What is so magical about the number twenty-one? One day you're not legal and the next you are."

"In six months, you'll find out."

She put her hands on her hips. "Are you going to stand there and tell me you and Tobias never took a drink until you were twenty-one?"

Deacon drank the punch and handed the empty cup to Skyler. "I believe this falls under the 'Do as I say, and not as I do' rule."

She shook her head. "You're such a hypocrite."

Deacon put a hand on Skyler's shoulder. "You two have a good night. And say hello to your parents for me."

Skyler nodded. "Sure. Will do."

Deacon returned to Tobias, who had been joined by Angelina Heller. She'd been after Tobias since high school and one of the few women Tobias had never fallen in love with.

She got to her feet when he approached the bench. "Good evening, Deacon."

"Angelina. Thanks for keeping Tobias company."

"Anytime."

"But we've got some business to attend to, so..."

"Oh, of course." She put a hand on Tobias' arm. "Save me a dance?"

Tobias winked at her and gave her a thumbs up, then lost his smile when she left.

"She's so annoying."

"Because of her unwanted love for you?"

He looked at Deacon. "I know what you're getting at. But it's totally not the same thing."

"Right." He pulled Tobias to his feet. "You keep telling yourself that."

As they headed for the front of the building, Deacon took out his phone and called the driver. They waited five minutes for him to arrive, then Deacon put Tobias in the front seat.

Tobias smiled. "I never get to sit in the front. It's always Mother or you."

"We're a pecking order, inside a pecking order. Everyone has a role to play."

"Yeah. I'm still trying to figure out what my role is." Deacon started to close the door, and Tobias put a hand on it. "Wait, I remember. I'm the runner up. The second son. The spare heir."

"You're not a spare. Mother has no intentions of leaving everything to me."

"How do you know?"

"I helped her write her will." He closed the door. "Go home and get some sleep. And no more rum. We need to be on the field at eight tomorrow morning."

Tobias gave him a mock salute as the car drove off.

Chapter Five

"What he doesn't know, he can't disapprove of."

"*What he doesn't know, he can't disapprove of.*"

With everything running smoothly, Deacon found himself with nothing to do. He wandered out to the garden and made his way to a spot concealed by a circle of Italian cypress with just a small opening to walk through. The ground had a brick covering with moss growing in the spaces between them. There were curved benches around the edges, separated by replica Greek sculptures, which seemed out of place in rural Texas. There was a large round table with six chairs, in the middle of the space.

Deacon was glad he found it empty. He leaned against the table and put a foot on one of the chairs. When he heard, "Oh, sorry," he looked up to see Cassidy coming through the opening.

"Don't be. It's a public space."

She walked closer to him. "Did you run out of waiters to torment?"

"Seems everything's in order."

"Bummer. What's a poor rich cowboy to do?"

"Hide out. It's the next best thing to being an asshole."

She smiled. "I probably shouldn't have called you that."

He nodded. "You could've waited a little while until you were sure the label fit."

"I'll remember that next time."

"If you're looking for your intended, I sent him home."

"Is he being punished?"

Deacon got to his feet. "No. Tobias has a tendency to overindulge sometimes."

She sat on a bench. "Are you saying he's an alcoholic?"

"No. But he's doing his damnedest to get there."

"Is he drowning out demons?"

"No. It's more for medicinal purposes." Deacon sat on the next bench over. The statue between them was of a scantily dressed woman and it partially obscured his view of Cassidy.

"He said something about a horse accident."

Deacon nodded. "He had a fall a few years back. Fractured his leg in a couple of places. It's never really healed properly."

"Has he tried any non-medical or alcoholic remedies?"

"Such as?"

"Yoga? Meditation? Physical therapy?"

Deacon smiled and stood again. "I'll let you try to convince him of that once you're married."

She stood, too. "Married? Now I'm engaged?"

Deacon walked around the circle, pausing to look at the sculptures before coming back and stopping a few feet in front of Cassidy. "You know, if this was Victorian England, you and I would have to get married."

"Why?"

"Because we're alone here without an escort."

"Goodness."

"So, be glad you're living in Texas in the twenty-first century."

"I don't know if it's all that different. Seems I'm engaged to someone I just met a few hours ago."

Deacon laughed. "Like I said earlier, he'll get over it."

Cassidy walked to the table and leaned against it. "How often has Tobias been in love?"

Deacon thought for a moment. "Four times."

"That doesn't seem too excessive."

"This year."

"Four in nine months? Suddenly I don't feel so special."

"He insists you are."

"How?"

Deacon folded his arms across his chest. "Let me put this politely. None of the other women teach high school English."

"And how about you, Deacon? Why aren't you settled down with a wife and a few kids? Seems your role as the first son would expect that."

"Not for me. Never going to happen."

"That sounds...finite." She cocked her head. "You know, if you backed off a little on the whole snobbish asshole vibe, there's probably a woman or two that might find you appealing."

"I haven't always been a snobbish asshole. I just found that the only thing appealing to those couple of women was my ranch and the money that comes with it."

She shook her head. "I'm sorry you're so jaded. I truly feel there is someone out there for everyone. But you have to be open to it."

"Should I go do some yoga and meditate about it?"

Cassidy pushed away from the table. "Not everyone is interested in money."

"I've yet to meet one."

She walked to him and held out her hand. "Cassidy O'Hare."

He took her hand and held it for a moment. "That's easy for you to say. You're going to inherit your grandfather's ranch someday."

She retrieved her hand and took a step back. "How do you know that?"

"It's my job to know what's going on in my small, snobbish world. Your father and your grandfather haven't spoken in twenty-seven years. I doubt he's going to leave his fortune to him. Is that why you moved here? To learn the business while he's still around?"

Cassidy returned to the bench and sat. "I moved here because I couldn't breathe in Austin anymore. I was raised by a flighty mother who didn't believe in rules or plans. She always followed her muse wherever it wanted to take her. So my father felt he needed to counteract that with being the serious disciplinarian. I never realized how trapped I was in their weird dynamic until I went to college. Once I graduated, I couldn't see going back to it."

Deacon grinned. "Is this where I'm supposed to feel sorry for you?"

She stood again. "I don't want you to feel anything for me. I was just answering your question."

"Right. Sorry." He glanced toward the exit. "I should probably go check in with my mother."

"It's like you enjoy being an asshole."

"I'm my father's son."

"Your father was an asshole, too?"

"No. He wasn't. My father was a great man, who died too soon and left the Starlight without a captain."

"So, you had to take on the mantle?"

"Yeah." He headed for the gap in the trees. "Enjoy the rest of the evening, Cassidy."

Cassidy dropped back down on the bench and sighed. Deacon Carmichael was an extremely frustrating man. Yet she was drawn to him. She liked being challenged. She thought about Tobias. He was funny and possibly sweet. Though the drinking was a bit of a red flag. He was also just as handsome as Deacon. But he wasn't Deacon. Tobias was apparently a troubled man who used humor and alcohol to deal with his pain. Tobias would be a project she wasn't prepared to take on. Deacon was a man with the weight of the world on his shoulders. Or at least the weight of the Starlight Ranch. He wasn't a project. He was a dead end.

With a sigh of resolve, Cassidy left the little center of peace and returned to the party.

Abby and Skyler were at a table discussing whether English show events or western rodeo events were more demanding. Abby competed in the high school rodeo events of barrel racing and pole bending. And she and Tanner had been team roping for a few years together at local non-professional events. Skyler participated in show jumping and Eventing when he was younger. But had switched to polo in college.

Abby smiled at him. "Let's just agree they both take their own set of skills."

He leaned back in his chair. "Okay, Ms. Rodeo Queen."

"Three years in a row."

"Are you riding tomorrow?"

"I'm going to run the barrels and Tanner and I are going to rope."

"I'll have to come watch."

She smiled at him. "You're going to slum with the rodeo people?"

"Hey, I'm still a cowboy at heart."

She studied him for a moment. "I don't suppose you'd like to chase the hounds tomorrow morning?"

"I always wanted to do that. My parents wouldn't let me. They were afraid I'd get hurt and ruin their championship goals for me."

"Well, it seems like a Harvard man should be able to do whatever the hell he wants to do."

He nodded and sat up in his chair. "You're right. Aren't the teams already set, though?"

"All you have to do is show up. We can be on my brothers' team."

"All three of them?"

"No. Just Deacon and Tobias. Tanner wants to save his horse for the other events on Sunday."

"You sure they're not going to have a problem with me joining in?"

"Probably. They're going to have a problem with me joining too. But that's not going to stop me."

He grinned. "I'll be there."

"I was also thinking about going to the barn dance tomorrow night. There might be some cowgirls there looking to cozy up next to that handsome Fremont boy, freshly home from Harvard."

"Hmm. Might be interesting."

"I'm going to be meeting someone there. But if you show up, I'll introduce you around. Of course, you might know some of them."

"I'll keep it in mind." He leaned back in his chair again. "Doesn't seem like the type of thing your brother would be okay with."

"What he doesn't know, he can't disapprove of."

"I like your style, Abby." He scowled. "Dammit. Here comes my mother."

"She can't have a problem with you spending time with a Carmichael."

"I'm sure she's thrilled. But she does have some reservations about your wild nature." He gave her a wink and Abby smiled. Skyler got to his feet. "Mom."

"Skyler, there you are." She looked at Abby. "Sorry to interrupt, dear, but I need to steal him away for a while."

"Of course. I didn't mean to monopolize all of his time."

"He's just back, you know. There are quite a few people who'd like to say hi."

"I'll be there in a minute, Mom."

"Okay, honey." She glanced at Abby before leaving the table.

Abby giggled. "It's like we're prized possessions being auctioned off to the highest bidder."

"Tell me about it."

"So, am I going to see you tomorrow morning?"

He smiled, then nodded. "If they don't have me married off by then."

Abby watched him go. He was cute. But she wasn't interested. At least not in the way her mother wanted her to be. He might be fun to hang out with, though. She hoped he showed up tomorrow. She could use a friend who seemed to share her views on the Texas Ten's way of doing things.

Chapter Six

"It's not a race until someone ends up in the mud."

Deacon and Tobias were on their horses, waiting for the chase to start. There were four teams, and each would follow their own set of two hounds. The scents had already been laid out on four trails leading to an open field. The races often ended in a full-out gallop across the field to the finish line at the far end of it. You could have as many riders in your group as you wanted, but generally they were made up of two to five riders.

This year, Deacon and Tobias were the only riders on their team. When they saw Cassidy riding toward them, Tobias smiled.

"You came."

Deacon shook his head. "What are you doing here?"

"Tobias said it was open to anyone."

"Technically, yes. But it's not a Sunday ride in the park."

"I realize that. Can I be on your team?"

Deacon glanced at Tobias, who was grinning. "Um..."

Tobias interrupted him. "Of course you can. The more the merrier."

Abby rode up with Skyler. "Then you won't mind if we join you, too?"

Deacon looked at her. "Abby. You could get hurt."

"So could you."

He squinted at her, then looked at Skyler. "Fremont."

"Carmichael."

Deacon raised an eyebrow at Skyler's English saddle, breeches, and riding boots.

Skyler smiled at him. "I've spent the last eight years in an English saddle."

"Right." Deacon adjusted his hat. "Fine. Whatever. Just don't expect me to babysit any of you. We only need one rider to pass the finish line to win."

"My dear brother. You don't need to worry about us keeping up."

Deacon knew they were both good riders. Abby had been on a horse since she was three. Skyler was a champion show jumper, and currently a polo player, he had guts if nothing else. But he wasn't sure about Cassidy.

Cassidy glanced at him as though she knew what he was thinking. "What's the prize if we win?"

"*When* we win. A bottle of Glenfiddich."

"Scotch? The grand prize is a bottle of scotch?"

"Yes. It's tradition."

She leaned toward Tobias. "Is he always so grumpy in the morning?"

"Not just the morning."

Deacon glanced at them. "You know I can hear you, right?"

Cassidy ignored him and turned to Tobias. "So, how does this work?"

"In about five minutes, they'll let the hounds go. We'll be following those two." Tobias pointed at two bloodhounds who looked too relaxed to put up much of a chase.

"They look pretty subdued."

"Don't worry. They haven't gotten a whiff of the scent yet."

"Okay. So we follow them."

"Over hill and dale. Through trees. Over trees. Across creeks. Up hills. And down the other side."

She smiled. "Sounds exciting."

"Basically ride like the devil's chasing you."

"Got it."

Deacon looked at her. "Have you ever ridden like the devil's chasing you?"

"You don't need to worry about me, Deacon."

He sighed, but didn't respond.

The hounds were given the scent and a horn sounded alerting the riders. The dogs were let loose, and the riders took off after them.

Deacon glanced back at Cassidy. She was riding next to Tobias and looked like she knew what she was doing. Abby and Skyler came up next to him.

Abby glanced at Deacon. "Our hounds are kind of slow."

"Give them a minute. They're picking up the trail."

The hounds suddenly darted off and the five of them chased after them. They entered a stand of old oaks and had to slow down as they wove their way through the low-lying bows and oversized roots. At one point, the only way through was to make a three foot jump over a fallen tree. Deacon cleared it, followed by Abby and Skyler. Cassidy jumped next, followed by Tobias.

When they cleared the trees, they crossed a small meadow and came to a creek. They slowed again through the rocky creek bed, and Deacon looked back at Cassidy. She was right behind them, but Tobias was lagging behind.

Deacon turned. "Keep going. I'll be right back."

Cassidy looked back at Tobias, before continuing across the water.

Deacon got to Tobias, turned his horse, and followed alongside of him.

"Are you okay?"

"Yeah. That jump tweaked my leg. I'll be okay in a minute. Go ahead. I'll catch up."

"You sure?"

"Yep."

Deacon nodded and caught up to Cassidy, Abby, and Skyler.

When the dogs split up, Cassidy looked at Deacon as he came up beside her.

"Who do we follow?"

"Just pick one. They're all going to the same place."

She glanced back at Tobias. "Is he okay?"

"Yeah. He'll catch up."

"Shall we chase the red one?"

"Sure."

They took off after the dog, while Abby and Skyler followed the other one. The big red dog led them into another stand of twisty oaks. The trees were so thick they had to slow down to a walk.

"Are you sure Tobias is okay?"

"Yeah. He really shouldn't ride at all. But he loves this, and he does it every year, even though he pays for it for a couple weeks afterwards."

"His leg's that bad?"

"Yeah." Deacon headed for a low-lying branch and jumped his horse over it. When he heard a yelp behind him, he looked back and saw Cassidy's horse on one side of the tree and Cassidy on the other, sitting in a patch of mud.

He rode back to her and dismounted. He knelt next to her. "Are you okay? Are you hurt?"

"Just my pride." She tried to get up and Deacon took her arm. "Thank you." She frowned at her horse. "He decided at the last minute he didn't want to take the jump."

"I can lead him around."

She put her hands on her hips. "I really don't want him to get away with dumping me in the mud."

"Do you want me to take him over it?"

She studied him for a moment. "Would you mind?"

He smiled. "Not at all. I love putting horses in their place."

"Along with people?"

"That, too." He looked at her for a moment. "Although, with you, I'm a little confused. I can't quite figure out where you belong."

"Just go get my horse."

He climbed over the tree and took the horse's reins, before mounting him. He rode the horse back several yards and took a run at the jump. He felt the horse tense as they approached, but he didn't let him shy away. They cleared the jump and Deacon slowed him down and circled back to Cassidy.

"Thank you. Stanley can be a real brat sometimes." Deacon dismounted and handed her the reins. She patted the horse's neck, and got back in the saddle.

He looked up at her. "Are you sure you're okay?"

She nodded. "I hope that didn't slow us down too much."

"It's fine. The trees clear ahead. Then it's a straight shot across a meadow and up a bluff. We can make up some time."

"Okay. Let's go."

He smiled at her muddy pants. "It's not a race until someone ends up in the mud."

"I'm so glad it was me."

Deacon mounted his horse, and they rode to the edge of the trees. The meadow was a quarter mile wide. Cassidy looked at him, then dug her heals into her horse's side and took off.

Deacon raced after her and caught her as they got to the creek.

"Glad you could join me."

"You cheated."

"How so?"

"I wasn't aware we were racing."

"This is a race, right?"

"Yeah. But technically, we're racing the other teams, not each other." They crossed the river. "How'd you get to be such a good rider only visiting your grandfather during the summer? And not for several years."

"Believe it or not, they have horses in Austin, too."

He smiled. "Okay. Fine. But it must be pretty hard to find riding like this around there."

"That's true."

Tobias came up behind them. "How the hell did I catch you two?"

Cassidy smiled. "I had a slight mishap. I wanted to go over the tree and Stanley didn't."

"Are you okay?"

"Yes. Just a bit muddy."

"It's not a race until somebody ends up in the mud."

Cassidy laughed and glanced at Deacon.

He nodded. "Let's finish this thing."

They climbed a bluff and when they came out on top, they could hear their dog on the other side. They took off at a gallop across the top, but slowed to go down the other side. The field with the finish line, was at the bottom of the bluff.

Deacon glanced at Tobias. "Are you up for this?"

"No, you two go ahead. I'll bring up the rear."

Deacon and Cassidy took off across the field. There were two other riders coming from the other side, just slightly behind them. Skyler and Abby came out of the woods and joined in on the race across to the finish line.

Deacon and Cassidy crossed the line first with the other four riders crossing too close to call. Tobias came across a moment later.

Cassidy looked at Deacon. "Did we win?"

"Damn right we did."

Tobias came up beside them. "Six years in a row."

Deacon shook hands with him. "The Carmichaels pull off another one. With the help of an O'Hare and a Fremont, of course." He looked at Abby. "Good job, Abigale."

"And you were afraid I was going to slow you down."

"I stand corrected." He smiled at Cassidy. "With you as well."

Cassidy smiled. "So now what?"

"We go back to the ranch."

"The same way we came?"

"No. There's a service road a quarter mile that way."

"We could've taken a road here?"

Tobias laughed. "It wouldn't have been nearly as fun."

They made their way to the dirt road and took their time on the way back. Abby and Skyler were out front a few yards and Deacon pulled in next to Tobias.

"Is that something I need to be worried about?"

Tobias smiled. "Brother, let our sister have some fun before she heads off to college."

Deacon sighed. "I suppose you're right."

"He seems to have grown up a lot since high school."

Deacon shook his head. "Once a trouble maker. Always a trouble maker."

Tobias frowned. "I was a trouble maker in high school."

"Which proves my point."

Tobias looked at Cassidy. "My brother loves me. He just hides it well."

They continued along the road for five miles, then came out in a pasture a half-mile from the house. When they arrived, they got a standing ovation from the crowd on the lawn in front of the house.

Mayor Patterson was the master of ceremonies for the weekend and he held up his hands to quiet the crowd.

"The Carmichaels pulled off another win. Congratulations!" He held up the bottle of Glenfiddich. "As is our tradition, the winning team of the Chasing of the Hounds is awarded a bottle of scotch. Back in the day, it wasn't nearly this expensive." He handed it to Deacon, who took off his hat and held the bottle up. The crowd cheered again. He put his hat back on and opened the bottle of scotch. He took a drink, then looked at Abby, who was next to him.

She cocked her head. "One drink won't kill me."

He shook his head and handed her the bottle. She glanced at him, then took a sip. She frowned and coughed as she handed the bottle to Skyler. He drank and passed the bottle on to Tobias, who took his swallow and handed it to Cassidy. She looked at the bottle for a minute.

Tobias grinned. "Next year you'll know better than to be last in line."

She laughed, then took a drink. She held it up, and everyone cheered again.

Deacon circled the others and came up beside her. She handed him the bottle, and he put the lid on it.

"Ready for some pancakes?"

"I'm so ready."

A few Starlight ranch hands came to take their horses. Everyone dismounted except Tobias.

He looked at Deacon. "I might need a hand."

Deacon went to him and gave him some assistance getting off the horse. Tobias held onto him for a minute, before letting go.

"I'm good."

"You sure?"

"Yep. Let's eat."

Chapter Seven

"You're not so bad yourself for a cowboy in breeches."

Cassidy looked at Tobias, Abby, and Skyler sitting at the table with her. Deacon had gone off to tell the cooks they needed pancakes for five. Tobias and Deacon looked quite different today, in cowboy mode. But she liked it. There was something about a man in a cowboy hat she couldn't quite resist. It was in her blood. Even though her father tried to leave his cowboy alter-ego behind, he'd passed it down to her. Her best childhood memories were on her grandfather's ranch. Now she was back, and she was happy it wasn't just a summer visit. She was here to stay. And now that she was getting to know the Carmichaels, things were getting interesting.

She was tired from the ride, but so glad she did it. It was exciting. Who wouldn't love racing through the wilderness with the Carmichael brothers? Now, after the ride, Tobias was his jovial self, but she could tell he was in pain. When Deacon returned, he had five glasses on a tray.

He set one in front of each of them. "Mimosas to go along with the pancakes."

Abby smiled. "For me too?"

"No. Yours is orange juice."

She started to complain, then seemed to think better of it. Deacon had also brought a bag with ice in it, and he handed it to Tobias, before sitting and holding up his glass. "To the best damn hound chasing team in Texas."

They all tapped glasses and took a drink.

Tobias reached for a spare chair and moved it closer so he could put his leg on it, then set the ice on his thigh. "I say, we all do it again next year."

Deacon looked at Abby. "Unfortunately, Abigale will be away at school."

She tilted her head at Skyler. "He's so cute. He thinks he's actually going to get his way."

Cassidy set her glass down. "Well, I don't know about these guys here, but I loved college."

Tobias laughed. "Are you saying you partied your way through college?"

Deacon looked at him. "No. That was you."

Tobias nodded. "I may have partied a little, but I still pulled off a 3.5 GPA."

Deacon nodded at Skyler. "How about you? What did you graduate with?"

"4.0."

"Impressive. Not easy to do. Even at Harvard."

Cassidy wasn't sure if that was a subtle dig, but Skyler ignored it. She shook her head. "Since I seem to be surrounded by smart people, I won't divulge my GPA. But what was yours, Deacon?"

He leaned back in his chair and took a sip of his mimosa.

Tobias put a hand on Deacon's shoulder. "He doesn't like to brag. But it's higher than anyone else at this table. You see. He actually went to college to study and learn stuff. Imagine that."

Abby shook her head. "How am I supposed to compete with that?"

Deacon smiled at her. "It's not a competition. But you've never backed down from a challenge. I know you can do better than Tobias did without too much effort."

Tobias frowned. "Hey."

Abby pointed her finger at Deacon. "I know what you're doing. I'm not going to fall for the 'look at it as a challenge, Abby' move."

Deacon shrugged. "I don't see how you think this subject is still up for discussion. Your tuition's been paid. You're enrolled. All you have to do is decide what classes you're going to take."

She folded her arms across her chest. "I'm surprised you haven't already picked them out for me."

Cassidy smiled at her. "Where are you going?"

"Southwestern." She glanced at Deacon. "He wanted to send me across the country to Yale just because he and Tobias went there. Like I'd even get in."

He smiled. "See, I can be reasonable. And of course you would've gotten in."

Cassidy picked up her glass. "You guys went to Yale?"

He nodded.

"I think I'm sitting at the wrong table."

Tobias smiled at her. "We won't hold the fact you didn't go to an Ivy League school against you."

"I think you just did." She looked at Abby. "I have a friend who went to Southwestern. She loved it."

"Where did you go?"

She glanced at Tobias. "The University of Dallas."

Tobias took a drink. "Okay. Change of subject. This conversation is boring."

Two waiters arrived with a platter of pancakes, and another of sausage and bacon. There was already a selection of syrups and butter in the middle of the table, along with plates, silverware, and napkins.

Tobias smiled at one of the waiters. "Can we get another round of mimosas please?" He glanced at Abby. "Virgin for her."

"Coming right up."

Abby frowned at him. "I thought you were supposed to be the fun brother."

"Fun maybe. But you're still my little sister."

Breakfast was enjoyable and Deacon made it through the meal without being a jerk. Tobias entertained them with tales from the last several races, and they all ate more pancakes than they should've.

When Tanner came up to the table, Tobias took his foot off the extra chair and nodded toward it.

"Take a load off, little brother."

Tanner sat down. "I wasn't sure if I'd be welcome at the winner's table."

Deacon held up his third mimosa. "You're always welcome, Tanner. I wish you'd joined us for the race."

Tanner picked up a stray piece of bacon. "Yeah. Me too. I'm regretting it now."

Tobias patted his back. "Next year, kid. You can fill in for Abby."

Abby glared at him. "I thought that subject was boring."

Tobias grinned. "It is." He drained his glass. "One more round?"

Deacon pushed away from the table. "Not for me. I've got to go have a talk with Esmeralda."

He stood, tipped his hat, and left the table.

Cassidy watched him, then looked at Tobias. "Esmeralda?"

"His horse. His jumper. She hasn't been performing too well the last few days. He's going to go psych her out, or threaten her. One of those." He waved at a waiter. "He spends way too much time talking to his horses."

Tanner laughed. "Yeah. But it works."

"Says the man, who also spends too much time talking to horses."

Abby stood. "I'm going to take a really long shower."

Tanner looked up at her. "Okay. But then meet me at the corrals. I want to practice another time or two."

"Tanner. We've got this. We're going to win."

He grinned. "Okay, fine."

Texas show jumping, as they liked to call it locally, was a lot less formal than traditional show jumping. It was held in an outdoor arena and the jumps resembled fallen trees, creeks, fences, and stone walls. The riders could use either western or English saddles, with the choices evenly distributed between the ten riders.

Deacon was on Esmeralda and for jumping, he preferred an English saddle. He had a long talk with her and had high hopes of making all the jumps. When he rode up to Cassidy and Tobias, she seemed surprised by his semi-English style of breeches and knee-high riding boots. Of course it could have been the contrasting denim shirt and cowboy hat that threw her.

"Looking good, Mr. Carmichael."

He nodded. "Thank you." He patted Esmeralda's neck. "I just hope this lady decides to cooperate."

Cassidy ran her hand down the horse's long mane. "She's beautiful."

"She used to be Tobias'. And he was a much better jumper than I'll ever be. I think she knows that. That's why she gets testy with me sometimes. She figures she knows better than me."

Tobias patted the horse's rump. "You be good for Deacon. We don't want to embarrass ourselves."

Deacon left to join the other riders, and Cassidy looked at Tobias. "Do you miss it?"

"More than you know. She damn near took me to the Olympics."

"I didn't know. You must've been really good."

He shrugged. "It wasn't meant to be."

"How long ago did you get hurt?"

"Four years ago. Esmeralda took a bad hop on one of the jumps. We both went down, and she landed on top of me. I was in a coma for three days."

"Oh my gosh. I'm so sorry. Your mother must've been going out of her mind."

"Actually, Deacon didn't tell her until he was able to have me transferred to a hospital here."

"I don't understand."

"Our father died after falling off a horse. She knows we need to ride to run the ranch. But she refuses to accept that it's even a possibility we might get up on a horse for the pleasure of it. The competition I fell in was in Colorado and Deacon stayed by my side every second. He may come off as an asshole sometimes. But when you need him, he'll be there."

"So your mother's not here today?"

"No. Even when we're all home safe, she doesn't want to hear about it. And she'll never come watch."

"That's kind of sad."

"It's just the way it is."

Abby and Tanner came up to them. "Has he ridden yet?"

Tobias shook his head. "No. He's up after this guy."

They found seats in the bleachers and watched the rider run the course. He looked good to Cassidy, but Tobias pointed out several things he did wrong. His score reflected Tobias was right.

"Okay. Here's Deacon."

"Is he good?"

"He's better than the last guy."

Deacon rode Esmeralda into the arena and circled it before lining up to run the course. To Cassidy, he looked fantastic. The horse seemed to fly over the jumps. Tobias watched silently, then stood and cheered when Deacon cleared the last jump. Cassidy, Abby, and Tanner stood too, along with most of the people in the stands.

Cassidy leaned toward Tobias' ear. "Did he do good?"

"That was an excellent ride."

After two more riders finished, Deacon had the best score with only one fault point. The last rider was Skyler.

Abby clapped for him as he came onto the field, and Tobias frowned.

She shrugged. "He's my friend."

"He's also damn good."

Skyler's ride was flawless, and he earned zero faults, giving him a perfect score.

"Dammit."

Abby clapped and stood to cheer for Skyler. Cassidy joined her, then Tanner stood too.

Tobias stayed seated.

The three top riders came back onto the field, with Skyler in first and Deacon in second. During the gala weekend of events, no trophies or ribbons were awarded. Instead, the money that would've been spent on them, along with all the entry fees, were donated to a local charity. So the riders received a handshake from the mayor and a round of applause for their efforts.

A few minutes later, Deacon came out, leading Esmeralda. Tobias shook his hand as the others clapped for him. When Skyler came up behind him, Deacon turned and nodded.

" I he man of the hour."

Skylar shook with him. "You're not so bad yourself for a cowboy in breeches."

Abby gave Skyler a hug. "You were fantastic."

Skyler shook his head. "Six years of formal training and I barely beat your brother."

Tobias laughed. "It's hard to beat a Carmichael, Fremont."

Deacon headed for the barn, and Cassidy caught up to him.

"That was quite impressive. I take it your talk with Esmeralda paid off."

"She did well. Just barely clipped that fourth rail."

"Is that how you got the fault?"

"Yeah." He smiled. "She actually did better than I thought she would."

"Well, like I said. Impressive."

"Thank you." They reached the barn, and he removed the bridle and tied Esmeralda to a post.

"But of course, you jump." He grinned. "Oh wait, no you don't."

Cassidy nudged his shoulder. "Shut up. That was all Stanley. I made the jump just fine."

Deacon laughed. "You're right. You did."

"So, what's next?"

"There are some more horse events, and the auction. Then later the barbecue."

"So, we're booked for the rest of the afternoon?"

He looked at her. "Looks that way. Thanks for hanging out with us today."

"Of course. I'm having fun."

"Good."

"And thanks for trying to talk up college this morning at breakfast. Abby is dead set on not going." He released the girth.

"At the risk of bringing back grumpy Deacon. Why are you so dead set on her going?"

He stopped and looked at her. "Because it was my father's dream that all of his children went to college. Neither he nor my mother went. And they both regretted it."

"Why didn't they go? Surely your father's family had the money to send him."

"He kept putting it off. Too much work to do on the ranch. Too many rodeos to attend. Then he met my mother, and he didn't want to leave her. They met when she was seventeen, married as soon as she was eighteen, and had me a year later."

"Wow."

"He was a bronc rider. But he stopped when I was a baby."

"Okay. Abby needs to go to college for your dad."

Deacon nodded, then unsaddled Esmeralda.

"But..."

He pulled the saddle off and looked at her. "There really is no room for a but, here."

"But if it's going to make her miserable."

"I appreciate your...input. But it's really none of your business."

"You're right. It's not." And Deacon, the asshole, is back.

Chapter Eight

"Very conservative wealthy cowgirl."

Cassidy promised her grandfather she'd go to the auction with him, so she excused herself from the Carmichaels, and went home to change. She'd promised Tobias to meet back up with him at the barbecue.

While she showered and got dressed, she thought about the race that morning. Riding with Deacon had been quite exciting. And even though she told him and Tobias she was a good rider, she'd never ridden anything quite as challenging as the Texas Chasing of the Hounds race.

She hoped Tobias was okay. He seemed to be uncomfortable during breakfast and while they watched Deacon's event. She felt bad for him and was sorry there wasn't anything that could help him. She could tell he missed jumping.

She dressed appropriately for the auction in clothes befitting the granddaughter of a wealthy rancher. Winston wasn't nearly as well-off as the

Carmichaels. He had a third of the land and he didn't run cows. He made his money from breeding and selling horses.

Cassidy was dressed in beige slacks and a light blue cotton shirt with pearl buttons. She had a blue houndstooth scarf around her neck and a small formal cowboy hat made from dark blue suede. She slipped on knee high riding boots, before going downstairs to her grandfather.

"My dear, you look absolutely stunning."

"Thank you, Granddad. Do I look like I'm in the market for a horse or two?"

"You look like you could buy the whole lot."

They drove to the auction and Cassidy wondered if the Carmichaels would be there. They spent an hour looking at the horses, and Winston picked a few he wanted to bid on. Then he told Cassidy to find one she liked. He helped her read their pedigrees, check their legs for hidden problems, and watch their stride when they walked. She chose a white mare with a gray main and tail.

"If that's the one you want, then we'll bid on her."

"Thank you, Granddad."

"We won't go crazy, though. There is a cap to what I'll spend on her."

"Of course. I understand. You know what she's worth. I'll follow your lead."

The auction was exciting and Winston lost his first horse and won the second. As Cassidy's choice was being brought out, she spotted Deacon across the lot from them. He tipped his hat, and she gave him a wave. He was back in jeans and cowboy boots, which he seemed more comfortable in. Although, he seemed comfortable in his suit at the gala, too. Or maybe he just wore it so well, he gave off the illusion of comfort. She assumed he'd look good in anything. *Or nothing.* She smiled at the thought.

Winston looked at her. "What's on your mind, child?"

"I'm just glad to be here, Granddad."

"You're a blessing for sure. Let's win you this horse."

When the bidding opened, someone else made the first bid, then Winston made his. Across the lot, Deacon lifted his paddle and raised the bid. Cassidy cocked her head at him, then looked at her grandfather.

"What do you think?"

"I think I don't want to try to outbid Deacon Carmichael. He has much deeper pockets than I do. I'm sorry, dear. If he's in. I'm out."

One more bidder tried, but the horse went to Deacon. His final bid was high and Cassidy was amazed someone could so easily pay so much for a horse.

From across the lot, Deacon nodded at Cassidy and Winston.

Winston shook his head. "That man's a smug one."

"That's one word for him." But Cassidy wouldn't really describe him as smug. He was confident, but not arrogant about it. He knew who he was, what he had, and what others thought about him. He seemed to have it all figured out. But yet, she felt she'd seen a touch of vulnerability, which he didn't want anyone else to see. Deacon was an interesting man.

When the auction was over, Winston ended up with two horses. As he left Cassidy to go pay for them, Deacon came over to her.

She shook her head. "You bought my horse."

"Sorry. She was too good to let go. But honestly, I didn't know Winston was interested until he bid. She's not what he usually goes for."

"That's because he was buying her for me."

"Oh. Sorry."

"It's fine. I have a perfectly good horse."

"Stanley? I guess as long as you're not jumping."

"Will you give that a rest, please? Besides, you got him to jump the tree."

He took a step back and looked at her outfit. "Very conservative wealthy cowgirl."

"Do you like it?"

"I don't know. I think I'm partial to muddy jeans."

"Is Tobias with you?"

"No. He's taking the rest of the day off. He's probably half-way through a bottle of rum right about now."

"He was going to take me to the barbecue."

"Well, I'm not nearly as fun or charming, but I'll escort you if you'd like."

She folded her arms across her chest. "Only if you promise not to be...you."

"Who else am I supposed to be?"

She raised an eyebrow. "I guess since this isn't a Carmichael event, you might be a little less intense."

"I'll try my best not to be intense."

"Okay. Where's it at?"

"The fairgrounds. I'll pick you up at six."

"Oh. Okay. How proper."

"The parking is hell. It's a matter of convenience, not chivalry."

"Well, a girl can hope."

Winston returned and shook hands with Deacon. "You got yourself a good horse."

"Yeah. Sorry. If I'd known you were trying to get it for Cassidy, I would've been a little less enthusiastic."

"No worries. Polite bidders go home empty handed."

Cassidy was waiting on the front porch when Deacon drove up in his Jeep Cherokee. When she got into the vehicle, he looked at her more casual outfit of jeans and a t-shirt under a light jacket.

She smiled. "Better?"

"A little too clean. But yeah."

"Well, since we're going to a barbecue, I'll probably end up with sauce on me before the night is over."

"That should work."

"How's Tobias?"

"He's depressed Tobias tonight. I'm never sure which one I'm going to get when he settles into a bottle."

"I'm sorry. How often does he get like this?"

"Depends on his pain level. I keep telling myself it's better than pain killers. But sometimes I wonder."

She buckled her seatbelt. "Sorry. I just brought the mood down considerably."

"I worked with your horse a little this afternoon. She's got a lot of spirit."

"My horse? I believe if she was my horse, she'd be in my grandfather's barn."

"I actually feel kind of bad I outbid him. If you really want her, tell Winston I'll sell her for his highest bid."

She turned in her seat. "That's very generous of you, but I'm afraid you'd lose quite a bit of money. Granddad dropped out pretty early."

Deacon shrugged. "It's only money. Think about it. Of course, the price goes up once she has some training."

"What do you want to do with her?"

"I need a good jumper. Esmeralda has never really performed for me like she did for Tobias. I believe she misses him."

"That's sweet. And sad."

"Horses make connections just like people do." He glanced at her before pulling into the parking lot at the fairgrounds.

Cassidy looked at the crowded lot. "Wow, you weren't kidding."

"This is the most popular event of the weekend, with the chili cook-off tomorrow coming in at a close second."

They drove around for a few minutes before finding a spot that seemed a little too small for Deacon's Cherokee.

She looked at him as he pulled past it then prepared to back into the space. "Looks a little tight."

"I've got it. Why don't you get out though, before I pull in?"

She got out of the vehicle and moved away as he backed into the spot, leaving little room on either side of it. He opened his door.

"Good thing I didn't eat lunch." He squeezed out and joined her.

"Did you really miss lunch?"

"Ruthie forced an apple on me. But that was it."

"Ruthie?"

"She keeps the Carmichael home clean and our stomachs full."

"I see. That must be quite a job."

"It keeps her busy."

"She practically raised Tanner and Abby, too. They were only seven and ten when my father died and my mom...never quite got over it."

"I'm sorry."

"She can function at a social level as the matriarch of the family. But the day-to-day stuff, she doesn't have the heart for, and she spends a lot of time in her room. She reads, she paints, and she writes in a journal. I'm not sure what the hell she writes about, but she has a stack of them. She's always at dinner though. And she insists the rest of us are too."

"So you really have had to carry the mantle as the head of the ranch and family."

"Since I was twenty-three." He smiled at her. "You're determined to bring the mood down tonight, aren't you?"

"I'm sorry. No more talk about family or sad horses."

"Deal." They stopped at a long row of food booths. "Okay. You have a serious decision to make now. We have the classic hamburgers and hot dogs. Ribs, both beef and pork. Pulled pork or chicken sandwiches. A half of a chicken roasted. And at the end, Bill's barbecuing T-bones."

"Wow. How do I decide? What are you going to have?"

"I usually go for the baby back ribs."

She looked at him. "I've always wondered about the origin of those. Are they from baby pigs?"

He laughed. "No. They're the upper ribs. The farthest away from the spine."

"Okay. I'll have those."

He took her arm, and they got in line behind five other people. Deacon said hi to several people passing by and Cassidy noticed they were mostly women.

"Aren't you popular with the ladies of Connelly!"

"People tend to gravitate to something they can't have."

"Like the unavailable Deacon Carmichael?"

"Yeah."

They reached the counter and Deacon looked at Cassidy. "Can you eat a whole slab?"

"I don't know."

He looked at the man behind the counter. "Walt, we'll take two slabs and..." He glanced at Cassidy again. "Corn?" She nodded. "And corn on the cob."

"How about some sourdough bread?"

"Got to have that." Deacon paid for the meals, then tucked a twenty in the tip jar. A few moments later, Walt handed them their plates.

Cassidy checked it out. "Wow. This is a lot of food."

They searched for an empty table and saw one being vacated. They made their way over to it and sat down. There was a roll of paper towels in the middle of the table, along with a bottle of barbecue sauce, salt and pepper, and packaged wet wipes.

Deacon set his plate down. "How about something to drink?"

"Sure."

"What do you want?"

"Um..." She noticed a booth selling beer. "A beer?"

Deacon grinned. "Beer it is."

There was quite a line, and Cassidy watched Deacon go to the front of it and have a conversation with the man in the booth. He walked away with two beers and she smiled at him.

"How'd you manage to jump to the front of the line?"

"I paid for everyone's beer."

"That's one way to do it." She liked how confident he was. Again, he wasn't arrogant, he just knew who he was and what he wanted. Then he did what he had to do to get it.

He sat down. "Dig in."

"I don't know where to start."

They started eating, and it was so good, there wasn't much time for conversation. The was a lot of mmming and finger-licking, but both of them managed not to drip any barbecue sauce on their clothing.

Two-thirds of the way through her ribs, Cassidy had to stop. "Oh my gosh. I can't eat another bite." She sat up straight in an effort to make room for all the food she ate, then drank her last sip of beer.

"You saved room for pie, right?"

"There's pie?"

"Of course there's pie."

When Tanner and Abby approached, Tanner nodded at the table. "Mind if we join you?"

Deacon smiled. "Sure. Squeeze on in."

Tanner sat next to Deacon and Abby sat next to Cassidy. They both had pulled pork sandwiches, with chips and soda. The sandwiches were so big and full of meat they were hard to pick up.

Deacon looked at them. "So, what are you two up to the rest of the evening?"

Tanner attacked his sandwich, chewed, then swallowed, before answering. "The guys and I are going to practice a little for tomorrow."

Abby smiled as she studied her sandwich for the best approach. "I'm just hanging out with some friends." She looked at Deacon as though she thought he might question her further, but he didn't.

"Sounds good. Have fun."

Abby watched him for a moment, then cocked her head at him. "Who are you?"

"What do you mean?"

"You're so agreeable."

He pointed at her. "I'm the guy who's going to kick your ass if you don't stop staring at me."

Tanner laughed. "There's the brother we know and love."

Deacon stood. "Okay. Who wants pie?"

Cassidy looked up at him. "I don't know if I can."

"Of course you can. What kind do you want?"

"Boysenberry?"

"Great choice." He looked at Tanner and Abby. "Apple, right?" They both nodded.

He left, and Tanner smiled at Cassidy.

"It's kind of weird hanging out with you outside of the classroom."

"It's been nice getting to know you this weekend."

Tanner blushed a little, and Abby laughed. "Seems you're quite popular with all the Carmichael men, Cassidy."

Tanner frowned at her. "Shut up."

Cassidy smiled. "I'm not sure how I wormed my way into your family so fast. I just met all of you."

Abby smiled. "Well, it seems to be a good fit. You make Deacon smile, which isn't easy to do."

"He does seem to be a bit..."

"Of a hard ass?"

Cassidy laughed. "No. I was going to say serious."

Deacon returned with four plates of pie and set them down. "Why do I get the feeling you all were talking about me?"

Abby took a piece of the apple pie. "Because we were."

Cassidy noticed he had boysenberry, too. "Is that your favorite, too?"

"Pie is my favorite. Any kind of pie."

Tanner pointed at him. "Except pumpkin." He looked at Cassidy. "He hates pumpkin pie."

Cassidy shook her head. "That's un-American."

"I know. Right?"

When Deacon frowned at something behind her, Cassidy turned to see Tobias approaching. He seemed a little unsteady on his feet. And he was still wearing his mud-spattered pants and boots from the morning race.

Tobias squeezed in next to Cassidy nearly knocking Abby off the other end of the bench. "Looks like I'm just in time for pie."

Deacon raised an eyebrow. "What are you doing here?"

"That's a hell of a question to ask your brother." He picked up a leftover rib and ate it, then licked his fingers. When he reached for Deacon's beer, Deacon moved it.

"Did you drive here?"

Tobias shook his head. "Caught a ride with one of the men." He scowled. "You know I don't drive when I'm...medicated."

"Let me take you home."

"I just got here." He smiled at Cassidy. "He's trying to get rid of me already."

Deacon stood and put a hand on Tobias' arm. Tobias pulled it away. "Don't touch me, brother."

Deacon looked at Abby. "Can you see that Cassidy gets home okay?"

"Of course." She and Tanner stood, and after a moment Cassidy got to her feet as well.

Tobias touched her arm. "I just wanted to apologize for not being here tonight."

"It's okay. Please let Deacon take you home."

Tobias looked at Deacon, then nodded his head. "I don't want to embarrass the family."

Deacon took his arm again. "You're not an embarrassment, Tobias."

Tobias looked at Deacon's hand, then glanced at Cassidy. "Sorry."

She touched his other arm. "Go home and get some sleep. I'll see you tomorrow at the rodeo."

She watched Deacon lead Tobias off, then looked at Abby and Tanner. "Is he going to be okay?"

Tanner nodded. "Deacon will take care of him."

Chapter Nine

"I'd expect no less from a Harvard man."

Faith made it quite clear she didn't want Abby going to the barn dance, stating there would be too many ruffians, hooligans, and drunken cowboys in attendance. Deacon also told her not to go. Both directives made her want to go all the more. So after telling her mother she was going to go hang out with some friends, Abby drove to the Three Cedars Ranch and parked her BMW SUV among the old pickups and motorcycles. She took off the jacket she was wearing over her sleeveless dress and pulled the elastic band from her hair, letting it fall loose. She ran her hands through it, then went inside.

After a few minutes, she spotted Butch and made her way over to him. He smiled when he saw her. "You came."

"I said I would." Butch seemed to already be a few beers in.

"You said you might." He put his arm around her. "Are you and Tanner entered tomorrow?"

"Team roping and Tanner is entered in a couple more events with his friends."

Butch laughed. "I'll be bull busting. I drew a bastard bull, so that sucks."

"Well, good luck." He smelled like beer and sweat and Abby didn't really want his arm around her.

"Can I get you a beer?"

"Um, sure." Anything to get his arm off of her.

Butch disappeared for a few moments, leaving Abby to introduce herself to his sketchy group of friends. They all had beers in their hands, and seemed a little too interested in her. Her mother's definition of those in attendance came to mind.

When Butch came back with two bottles of beer, he handed her one, and she took a sip. No one there seemed to care she wasn't quite legal. She'd tasted beer a few times, but not enough to know if she really liked it or not. And once, when she was sixteen, she tried some of Deacon's scotch. It was disgusting, which made her wonder how he drank it all the time. But Tobias' rum was even worse. She'd tried that too.

Butch took her hand. "Do you want to dance?"

She didn't really. But that is why she came. "Sure." They set their beers down on a table that had several other open bottles, along with an ash tray and a few stray packs of cigarettes. Smoking was something she hadn't tried, and didn't plan to. She found that to be disgusting. She did remember her father smoking cigars though. He'd sit on the porch and watch her and Tanner play in the yard at the end of the day. She didn't have a lot of memories of him, but that one stood out.

She and Butch made their way to the crowded dance floor. The whole place smelled like dust, sweat, cigarette smoke, and beer. A far cry from the gala, which smelled like perfume and men's cologne mixed in with the floral scent from all the flower displays. Abby didn't appreciate the difference. The gala may have been stuffy. But it sure smelled better. She was there to have fun, though, and she tried not to let it bother her.

She danced with Butch several times and he was pretty handsy. She didn't like to be groped. Especially by a smelly intoxicated cowboy. Her mothers description of ruffians, hooligans, and drunken cowboys was quite accurate. She had to tell Butch repeatedly to behave himself, and he mostly listened, but he didn't seem too happy about it. She wasn't sure what had happened to the cute cowboy she'd been flirting with over the last month. But it definitely wasn't the man she was dancing with. She tried to blame it on the beer. But maybe the alcohol was just bringing out his true nature.

Abby was offered several beers, but never finished any of them. Every table in the place was covered with bottles from empty to full. She kept setting hers down and forgetting where she left them. She also decided she didn't appreciate the taste of the beer, either. Maybe this whole drinking thing wasn't all it was cracked up to be.

When she spotted Skyler, she excused herself from Butch and his friends and worked her way through the crowd to get to him. He was a welcome sight. Clean, not drunk, and he smelled good.

"Hey."

He looked around the room, then frowned at her. "Do you actually find this entertaining?"

She shrugged. "Sure. Let me introduce you to my friends." She didn't want to admit to him she'd made a mistake by coming.

"Nah. I'm going to head out. This isn't really my thing. I just wanted to make sure you were okay."

"Are you sure you don't want to stay?" She really didn't want him to leave.

"Yeah. I'll see you around. Unless you want to leave with me. We could go get some pizza or something." It was tempting, but then she'd be admitting everyone was right.

She glanced back at Butch, who seemed pretty interested in who she was talking to. "I think I'll stay."

"Are you sure?"

"Yeah. I'll be fine."

He nodded, then headed for the exit. Abby watched him go, before making her way through the crowded room to Butch.

"Who was that guy?"

"A friend."

"What kind of friend?"

"Just a friend. Don't worry about him. Besides, he's leaving." She got a whiff of Butch again, and she briefly thought about changing her mind and leaving with Skyler. But Butch took her hand.

"Let's go get some air."

Some air sounded really good. "Sure. Sounds great." Anything was better than the inside of the barn.

He took her hand and led her through the crowd. They went through a side door to an area without any other people.

Abby looked around. "Oh. This is...cozy." She tried to ignore the red flags going off in her head.

Butch smiled at her. "Just the way I like it." He moved in close and put his arms around her. "I'm really glad you came."

Abby tried to push him away, but he tightened his grip. "Butch. Let go please. I want to go back inside."

"You said it was cozy." He leaned in and kissed her, and once again Abby tried to push him off.

"Butch, let go of me." The panic she initially felt, turned to anger.

When he leaned in for another kiss, Abby kneed him in the crotch. It was hard and right on target. He yelped, stepped away from her and grabbed himself. "You bitch. What'd you do that for?"

"I told you to let go of me." She stormed off around the building and ran into Skyler coming from the front of the barn.

"Whoa. What happened?"

She glanced over her shoulder. "Butch decided to get a little too friendly."

"Do you want me to go have a word with him?"

She took a breath to calm herself, then smiled. "No. I took care of it."

She started walking toward her car and Skyler caught up to her. "How?"

"Let's just say he won't be messing with me again."

Skyler cocked his head.

"And he might be a little sore riding his bull tomorrow."

He started laughing. "You're something else. Here I thought I was coming to rescue you. Seems you didn't need rescuing after all. Impressive Carmichael. Damn impressive."

She stopped walking and looked at him. "You were coming to rescue me?"

"Yeah. I got waylaid by a couple of cowgirls, and I saw your drunk friend take you out the side door. I know his type. He wasn't taking you out there for some fresh air."

"How do you know I didn't want to go out there with him for something other than fresh air?"

"Because I know you, too."

"You met me last night."

"We were in high school together for two years."

She was surprised he remembered her. "I was an underclassman. You were the school hottie. Why would you notice me?"

"You're pretty noticeable." He took her arm. "Come on. I'll take you home."

"I have my car."

"And you've been drinking."

"Not that much."

"You're twenty. Any beer is too much. Especially to drive home."

"Fine. I do feel a little fuzzy, I guess."

He put her in his car, which was a Porsche. It was a beautiful car, but a little out of place parked in front of a barn. He got in behind the wheel. "So, did you get cowboys out of your system for a while?"

"Yes." She looked around the car. "Pretty fancy wheels for a cowboy."

"It was my graduation present. I actually prefer my truck, though."

She turned in her seat and looked at him. She felt she had a comrade in Skyler. Like she could be honest with him and he wouldn't judge her. "It wasn't like I thought it'd be."

"A little too rough?"

"A little too stinky."

Skyler laughed. "Everyone has to slip out of their world once in a while to see how the other half lives."

"Do you ever?"

"Yeah. There was this place down the street from my apartment in Cambridge. A little hole-in-the-wall pub. I'd go there once in a while. Hang out and talk to people. It was interesting."

"That's hardly slumming."

"Close enough."

She put her face in her hands. "Man, Deacon is going to kill me. He's going to know I was there since I had to leave my car."

"Give me your keys. I'll have someone help me bring it to the ranch for you."

"Really?"

"Sure. We rule breakers need to stick together."

When they pulled into the driveway, Deacon and Tobias stepped off the porch. Tobias looked more put together and had changed out of his muddy jeans.

Abby sighed. "Dammit. Now I'm in trouble. The sheriff and his deputy are here."

"It's fine. They still don't know where you were."

They got out of the car and Deacon approached Abby. "Where the hell have you been?"

"Um…" She glanced at Skyler.

Deacon leaned in close to her. "Have you been drinking?" He looked at Skyler, but Tobias got to him first. Tobias stepped within a foot of Skyler and trapped him between himself and the car.

Deacon scowled at him. "Didn't we already have a discussion about you giving alcohol to Abby? It was just last night, I believe."

Skyler couldn't seem to get out any words.

Abby put a hand on Deacon as he headed toward Skyler. "It wasn't him. He brought me home because he didn't want me to drive."

Deacon looked at Skyler. "Is that true?"

"Yes." Skyler cleared his throat and managed to get out, "I just brought her home."

Deacon looked back at Abby. "Where were you?"

Abby looked at the ground for a moment. She'd never been able to lie to Deacon. "The barn dance." She looked up at him. "I'm not a child, Deacon."

"You could've fooled me. Why didn't Butch bring you home? Was he drunk, too?"

"I'm not drunk. I didn't even have a full beer."

Skyler finally seemed to find his voice. "Abby can take care of herself. She apparently took care of Butch right before we left."

Deacon studied Abby. "How so? And why did you need to?"

She took a breath. "He was getting a little forward, and I gave him a knee to the... you know what. Just like Tobias taught me."

Deacon looked at Tobias, who grinned. "Good girl."

Deacon still wasn't satisfied. "How forward did he get?"

"He just tried to kiss me. But I could tell it was a prelude to what he hoped would happen."

Deacon smiled, then pointed at her. "Well, I'm damn proud of you. But this doesn't mean you're not in trouble."

"What are you going to do, ground me? Deacon, I'm an adult. You need to stop thinking I'm sixteen."

He pulled her in for a hug. "I can't. You'll always be a kid to me. You're just going to have to learn to live with it." It was true, he was always going to think of her as a kid. But that was okay. As frustrating as he could be, Deacon always made her feel safe and loved.

Abby kissed him on the cheek, then went to Tobias and hugged him. "I couldn't ask for two better big brothers. But seriously guys, lay off just a little."

Deacon nodded. "I'll try."

Tobias laughed. "I'll try to make him try."

"Thank you. Now, if you gentlemen will excuse me, I've got to go wash this barn dance smell off of me." She smiled at Skyler. "Thanks for trying to rescue me. It was sweet."

Abby left the men, and Deacon looked at Skyler. "I guess I owe you an apology."

"No. It's fine. I don't have a sister. But if I did, I would've come to the same conclusion."

Tobias shook with him. "What were you doing at the dance?"

"I only went because she told me she was going. I thought I could keep an eye on her."

"Thank you."

"I was only there about ten minutes, but it was the right ten minutes. She was about to drive home." He dug in his pocket for Abby's keys. "Her car is at Three Cedars."

Deacon took the keys from him. "We'll go pick it up tomorrow." He thought for a moment. "Isn't that where Butch works?"

Tobias nodded. "Yeah. Maybe I'll come with you to pick up Abby's car tomorrow."

Skyler laughed. "I'm going to tell you guys this right now. You don't ever have to worry about me doing anything inappropriate with Abby. Between her skills and you two, I'll always be a perfect gentleman."

Deacon smiled. "I'd expect no less from a Harvard man. Although you Pilgrims do have a reputation for being a bit pretentious with the ladies. "

"Huh. The way I heard it. The ladies prefer a pretentious pilgrim over a slobbering bulldog."

Chapter Ten

"Relieved. Joyous. Exuberant."

When her grandfather knocked on her door while she was getting ready for the day, Cassidy opened it.

"Is everything okay?"

Winston smiled. "Yes, dear. I just wanted to let you know there's a Carmichael downstairs asking to talk to you."

"Okay. I'll be right down."

After her grandfather left, she realized she didn't even ask which one. She tried to determine if it mattered, but couldn't come up with an answer. It was too soon to tell.

She finished getting ready, then found Tobias in the entryway with his hat in his hands. He smiled when he saw her. He had a great smile.

"Good morning."

"Tobias. What are you doing here?"

He fingered his hat for a moment. "Can we take a walk?"

"Of course."

She took a jacket from a hook by the door and put it on as she went outside. They stepped off the porch and headed down the road. He looked better today, and didn't seem to be hungover.

"Is everything okay?"

He put his hat on. "I want to apologize for last night."

"Tobias, you don't—"

"Yes, I do. Sometimes, I let the alcohol get to me. Last night was one of those times. I'm sorry if I embarrassed you or made you think any less of me." Cassidy took his arm, and he went on. "I'm an idiot and I never should've left the house. I was sitting at home thinking about you being there with Deacon, and I talked myself into believing he was trying to make a move."

She smiled. "Deacon was a perfect gentleman. And you should know better than anyone. He seems to have no intention of making a move on any woman."

"I know that when I'm sober. Even if he hadn't sworn off women, he'd never do that to me. It was the rum demon talking in my ear."

"Okay. Let's forget about last night. Have you had breakfast?"

"No. I came right over without eating. Can I take you to town? The café has great biscuits and gravy."

"Mmm. Sounds good." They turned back toward the house. "I just need to get my things."

They drove to town and parked in front of the café. Once inside, they sat at a booth by the window. The waitress came with coffee, and Tobias ordered biscuits and gravy for them both.

Cassidy poured some cream into her coffee. "So, the rodeo today?"

"Yes. Abby is competing in the barrel races. It's kind of turned into a rodeo queen reunion. About half of the contestants are past royalty."

"That should be fun."

"Maybe. I'm not sure how they'll all get along. I think she's doing the pole bending too."

"And her and Tanner are doing something with roping?"

"Yes. Team roping. They're pretty good. Most likely they'll win. And of course, Tanner has decided to try his luck with a bronc."

"Oh, no."

"Deacon and I both tried to talk him out of it."

"He's young and adventurous."

"He is that." The waitress delivered their food, and Tobias picked up his fork. "Deacon and I have a quick mission this morning. But we can meet you at the rodeo. Abby's thing is around eleven."

"A mission, huh? Sounds mysterious."

"Abby snuck off to the barn dance last night and got a little tangled up with a cowboy. She put him in his place. But Deacon and I are going to pick up her car. Fortunately for us, but unfortunately for him, Butch works there, and will be there until the rodeo starts."

"I assume Butch won't be getting near Abby again, after you have a talk with him." She glanced at Tobias. "You're just going to talk, right?"

"Of course. We're not going to get into a tussle with a cowboy. Deacon, having a word with him, will be quite enough."

"I almost feel sorry for Butch."

"Don't. He's a son of a bitch."

Deacon and Tobias pulled up to the Three Cedars barn. Abby's car was one of a few others that didn't get driven home last night. They got out of Deacon's Jeep and went into the barn, and a young cowhand gave them a quick smile.

"What can I do for you fellas?"

Deacon looked around the barn. "We're looking for Butch."

The man finally seemed to realize who they were and he lost his smile. "You're the Carmichaels."

"Yeah. Where's Butch?"

"What do you want with him?"

"It's between him and us."

The two oldest Carmichael brothers standing shoulder to shoulder were an impressive sight, and the man swallowed hard. "Um... I'm not sure where he is."

Tobias stepped closer to him and gave him a smile. "Take a minute to think about it."

"Right. He's ah... I remember now. He's out loading up his horse."

Tobias nodded and took a step back. "Thank you."

They left the barn and followed the sound of men loading horses into a trailer. When they came around the corner, the cowboy on the ramp spotted them, then glanced inside.

"Butch?"

Butch came out of the trailer. "What?" He saw Deacon and Tobias and hesitated a moment, then assumed a look of defiance, before striding out of the trailer and approaching them.

"What can I do for you?"

Deacon stepped close to him, and Butch took a step back. "You'll be staying away from Abby from now on. I don't want you talking to her or speaking about.her. I don't want you to even think about her. Is that clear?"

Butch took a breath. "I don't know what you're talking about."

Deacon looked at Tobias. "He doesn't know what we're talking about."

Tobias moved next to Deacon. "Are you sure about that?"

"You guys can't come here and intimidate me."

Deacon smiled. "We're not here to intimidate you. We're just here to tell you to stay away from Abby."

Butch didn't quite want to give in. "What did she say happened?" He shook his head. "Nothing happened."

Tobias lowered his eyes to below Butch's belt line. "That's not what she said. And we're inclined to believe her over you."

"Fine. Whatever. She's a little too—"

"Too what?"

"Nothing. I'll stay away from her."

Deacon moved closer and put a hand on Butch's shoulder. "See that you do."

They turned and walked away from him, and when they got to the car, Tobias took Abby's keys from his pocket.

"I wish you would've let me punch the little punk."

"That would've brought us down to his level."

"Maybe. But it would've felt so good."

"We accomplished what we came for."

The little bastard was getting all cocky with us."

"Let it go, Tobias."

While Tobias went to check in with Abby, Deacon headed for the arena. He made his way to the bleachers and spotted Cassidy up near the top.

He climbed up to sit next to her, greeting people and shaking hands on his way up.

"Morning."

"Hi." She smiled at him. "Where's your brother?"

"He's giving Abby a last minute pep talk."

Cassidy laughed. "You and Tobias are like divorced parents raising their kids. He's the fun parent who takes them for ice cream and lets them eat dinner in front of the television."

"What's that make me?"

"The one who takes them to the doctor for shots and makes them go to bed on time."

He thought about it for a moment. "I guess that's truer than I'd like it to be."

She put a hand on his arm. "I'm kidding. You're great with Abby and Tanner. Maybe a little too controlling with Abby. But I think that's because you love her so much and it's hard for you to let her go."

"I told her last night, she'll always be a kid to me. And it's true. The fact that she's six months away from being twenty-one scares the hell out of me. I don't see how parents do it. How do you let your kid go off into the world and not worry about them every second of the day?"

"I don't think you do. Stop worrying, that is."

"I'm glad I'll never know. It's hard enough letting go of my sister and brother."

"How'd you feel when Tobias left for college?"

"Relieved. Joyous. Exuberant."

Cassidy tilted her head. "Come on, now."

He smiled. "I missed the hell out of him. We're seven years apart, but we were close growing up. Even more so after our father died, and Mother checked out. Just don't ever tell him I said so."

"I won't. I don't want to ruin your street cred."

Tobias joined them a few minutes later, and they watched as Abby dominated the field with her winning rides. She won first place in both events. Thirty minutes later, they watched her and Tanner take first in the calf roping.

Cassidy clapped for them while the men whistled and cheered. "My goodness. The Carmichael family is kicking some serious ass this weekend."

Tobias looked at Deacon. "Yeah. Just one second place among us."

Deacon shook his head. "Go to hell."

When it came time for the saddle bronc riding, the three of them went to stand at the fence. Tanner would be the third rider.

Cassidy looked at Tobias. "So, how does this work?"

"The rider and the horse are both scored. The horse is judged on how high he kicks his rear legs, and how far he drops his front end before he rears up. They're looking for the rider to rake the horse with his toes pointed out. And at no time can he touch the horse or himself with his free hand. He needs to look good while holding on with one rope, moving stirrups, and a crazy horse for eight seconds."

"Oh. So not difficult at all."

"Our dad was a bronc rider. And he was damn good. Mom made him quit when Deacon was a few years old."

Deacon nodded. "Yeah. Then he fell off a cow pony, and it killed him."

Tobias put a hand on Deacon's back for a moment. "When you get up on a horse, you're one bad fall from getting rolled on or kicked in the head."

Cassidy looked at Tobias and Deacon. "You guys never tried rodeo?"

Tobias laughed. "No. We went for the sissy stuff."

"Horse jumping isn't for sissies."

"Maybe. But it isn't riding a bronc."

The first rider didn't last his eight seconds. The second one did, but he didn't score very high. As Tanner was in the chute getting ready for his ride, Abby came to join them.

"I'm so nervous. I don't want to watch him. But I can't not watch him."

Deacon put an arm around her shoulder when Tanner gave the signal to open the gate.

"Here we go."

Tanner came out strong, and he'd drawn a good horse who was moving well. It was a rough ride, and Tanner did everything right. Deacon glanced at the countdown clock. Three seconds to go. As the clock hit eight, the horse made an awkward jump and Tanner flew over the bronc's head and landed hard in the dirt.

Abby gasped and tried to run to him, but Deacon held onto her. "Hold on. Give him a minute. And they've got to corral the bronc. Tanner wasn't moving, and as soon as two cowboys rounded up the bronc and got him out of the pen, Deacon and Tobias climbed the fence.

Deacon looked at Cassidy. "Keep Abby here." She nodded and took a hold of Abby's arm while he and Tobias ran across the arena to Tanner.

They knelt next to him as the standby paramedic joined them.

"Tanner. Talk to me, son,"

Tobias took Tanner's hand. "Come on, kid. Open your eyes."

Tanner stirred, then slowly opened his eyes. He tried to sit up, but all three men put hands on him.

"Did I make the eight seconds?"

Deacon smiled. "Yeah, kid. You stayed on for your ride."

The paramedic took a penlight and shone it in Tanner's eyes. "Take it easy there. Can you see me okay?"

Tanner nodded. "Yes, sir."

"Do you have pain anywhere?"

Tanner took a moment as he seemed to assess if there was any damage. "I don't think so. I just got the wind knocked out of me." He looked at Deacon. "I'm fine. Really."

"Give it a minute.

The medic took his arm. "Let's sit you up."

Tanner sat and closed his eyes for a moment. "I got my bell rung a little bit."

"Not surprising. You most likely have a bit of a concussion."

Tobias smiled. "You landed head first. Good thing us Carmichaels are so hard headed."

Tanner nodded. "I think I'm okay."

Deacon and Tobias stood and helped Tanner to his feet. Deacon patted his chest.

"How's that?"

Tanner nodded, then winced when he put weight on his left foot. "Shit."

The paramedic knelt and felt Tanner's ankle through his boot. When Tanner yelped, the man stood. "You better go to the clinic and have that looked at."

Tobias looked around the quiet stadium. All eyes were on them. "Okay kid, you ready for your victory lap?"

Tanner nodded again. "Just don't let go."

Deacon took his arm. "We got you."

They started walking toward the gate, and the stadium erupted in cheers and whistles. Tanner took off his hat and waved at the crowd.

Tobias laughed. "Does that help the pain a little?"

Tanner shook his head. "Nope."

Chapter Eleven

"Even Deacon Likes hanging out with you."

Deacon and Tobias helped Tanner out of the arena and through the gate, where Abby and Cassidy were waiting. Abby threw her arms around Tanner.

"Oh, my God. I thought you were dead." She stepped back a foot. "Are you okay?"

"Just a little shook. I'll be alright."

Tobias readjusted his grip on Tanner. "He messed up his ankle. We need to take him to the clinic."

"I'm coming with."

Deacon looked at her. "No sense in all of us going." He glanced at Cassidy and she nodded and took Abby's arm again.

"Don't you have a winner's ride to take?"

Abby looked at Tanner and he smiled.

"It's okay. Go ride with the rest of the rodeo queens."

"The bunch of bitches."

Deacon frowned at her. "Hey."

"It's true. They think they're all that because they were rodeo queen a hundred years ago."

Tobias laughed. "I'm almost sorry I'm going to miss this."

Deacon looked at him. "You can stay. We both don't need to go to the clinic."

Tanner sighed. "Can we just decide who's going and who's staying? I'd really like to go sit down."

Deacon laughed. "Sorry, kid." He looked at Tobias. "Stay here with Cassidy. I'll call you when I know what the damage is."

"Okay."

"And start thinking about what we're going to tell Mother."

Cassidy watched them go, then smiled at Tobias. "He'll be okay."

"Yeah. I know. He's tough. Let's go find out how he scored."

There was one more rider, and after he finished, the announcer called the names of the top three riders. Tanner took third.

Tobias whistled loudly. "That's my brother. Gets bucked off and still takes third place."

"How did that happen?"

"He stayed on long enough. After that, it doesn't matter what he does."

"Interesting."

Tobias took her hand. "How about we go have a beer and a hot dog?"

"A beer?"

"I can handle one beer."

Cassidy sighed. "Fine." After last night she wasn't totally convinced that was true.

He grinned and led her off to the food booths near the arena. He bought two beers and three hotdogs, then they sat at a table under a big oak tree.

Tobias smiled at Cassidy across the table. "So, pretty good day, huh?"

"Except for your brother being at the clinic right now."

Tobias shrugged. "He walked off the field. He'll be fine."

"So, you guys really aren't going to tell your mother what happened?"

He shook his head. "No. He's her baby. She'd lose it."

"What are you going to tell her?" She was having trouble reconciling the Mrs. Carmichael she met at the gala with the fragile woman her sons described.

"Deacon will think of something. She'll probably know he's lying to her. But she'd rather accept the lie than deal with the truth."

"Your father's death must have really hit her hard."

"She didn't leave her room for three years. Ruthie and Deacon raised us."

"How old were you?"

"Sixteen. Abigale was ten. Tanner was seven. I expect they barely remember him."

"Deacon said he was a great man."

Tobias nodded. "He was. Sure as hell didn't deserve to die the way he did." He took a bite of his hotdog and chewed it thoughtfully. "So, yeah. Mom doesn't want to know how Tanner got hurt."

Abby came up to their table with three rodeo queen sashes draped over her shoulder.

Tobias laughed. "That's a little overkill, isn't it?"

"No. I'm the only one with three of these. If they're going to be all snooty, I'll show them what's what."

Cassidy laughed. "Good for you."

"The ride's in ten minutes."

Tobias stuffed the end of his hotdog in his mouth and gave her a thumbs up.

Abby scowled. "You're gross. I think you're more immature than Tanner."

Cassidy shook her head, he seemed to be proud of the fact. "We'll be there, Abby."

When they got to the arena, Skyler was there and they went to stand with him.

Cassidy smiled. "Hi, Skyler."

"Hey." He nodded at Tobias. "Didn't want to miss Abby's big moment."

The rodeo queens came out one at a time and were introduced, then rode their horses around the arena. When Abby's name was announced along with being crowned three years in a row, Tobias and Skyler both yelled and whistled. She rode around the arena, looking beautiful in her black cowboy hat and her three sashes. She tipped her hat as she passed them, and Cassidy clapped and cheered.

Cassidy looked at Tobias. "Your sister is beautiful. You know that, right?"

"Yeah. That's why Deacon is so reluctant to let her grow up."

Skyler was grinning as he watched Abby head for the exit. "Gosh, she looks great on a horse." He glanced at Tobias and lost his grin. "I'm going to go say hi to her."

Tobias watched him go. "Hmm. Seems like we have a Skyler problem."

"Why is he a problem? He's really cute and he seems to like Abby." She watched Skyler greet Abby on the far side of the arena.

"Yeah. That's why it's a problem."

"Poor Abby."

He looked at her. "Why poor Abby?"

"You and Deacon are never going to relax and let her be."

He glanced toward Abby and Skyler. "We're just looking out for her."

"Seems like she can take care of herself."

Tobias laughed. "I guess Butch can attest to that."

"What did she do to him last night?"

"Kneed him right in the cohones."

Cassidy smiled. "Well then, Deacon doesn't need to worry about her taking care of herself."

He reached for her hand. "Have you ever given some guy the knee?"

"Only if he deserved it."

Tobias grinned. "That doesn't really answer the question.

"Just behave yourself and you won't have to worry about it."

"I'm always a perfect gentleman."

She smiled at him. "I find that a little hard to believe."

He put a hand on his chest. "I'll rephrase. I'm as much of a gentleman as the lady I'm with wants me to be."

"Okay. Good to know."

"I'm so glad I fell in love with you the other day."

She shook her head. "About that."

"No. No. Don't ruin it for me. Let me live in my little delusional world a little longer."

"So you admit it's delusional?"

"Is that what I said? No. That's not what I said at all." He kept hold of her hand and started walking. "Come on. I want to show you something."

"What? And Where?"

"It's not far. Right over here."

He took her behind the buildings to a stand of oaks, then ducked in behind a big one. They were out of sight of anyone who might pass by.

"Here we go."

"You wanted to show me a big oak tree?"

"No." He took both of her hands, then leaned in close. "I wanted to show you this." He kissed her softly. Then again, with a little more passion. He moved back a few inches and looked at her. Then he straighten and took a step back. "What do you think?"

"Do you want me to score you?"

He laughed. "No. Although if you wanted to. I guess I wouldn't mind."

She shook her head. "Never going to happen."

"The score? Or another kiss?"

"The score."

"So, the kiss was okay? I mean, you didn't mind me kissing you?"

"No. Tobias. I didn't mind."

He grinned. "Cool." He kissed her again, even more enthusiastically.

Cassidy put a hand on his chest. "Okay. Down boy. This is hardly the place for that kind of kiss."

"Fine. Will you come to the chili cook-off tonight?"

"Aren't you Carmichaels about tired of me?"

"Never. Even Deacon likes hanging out with you."

"Oh, that's flattering."

"It is. He doesn't like hanging out with anyone. He usually hates all this. But this weekend, I think he's actually enjoying himself."

Cassidy smiled. She hadn't minded that Tobias kissed her. But a part of her wished it had been Deacon. Was she like all the other women? Wanting someone she couldn't have simply because he was unavailable. She hoped not. She believed she saw him for who he really was. His serious and sometimes grumpy nature was just a mask, a cover for the young man who had to grow up too fast.

———— ❧❧ ————

While Deacon and Tanner were waiting at the clinic to see the doctor, a cute blonde, looking properly concerned, came through the door and rushed over to them.

Tanner looked surprised to see her. "Oh. Hey."

"Oh my gosh. I saw you fall. Are you okay?"

"Yeah. I'm fine. Just a little banged up."

The girl looked at Deacon. "Hi." Deacon nodded and she returned her attention to Tanner. "I thought for sure you were dead. Or at the very least, really hurt."

"No. Not dead."

She giggled. "I can see that."

The nurse called Tanner's name, and he looked at the girl. "I've got to go back now."

"Okay. I'll tell everyone you're okay."

"Thank you."

Deacon helped him back to the room and stood by while the nurse took his vitals. When she left them alone to wait for the doctor, he looked at Tanner.

"I thought you liked that girl?"

"Not her."

"That's not Hallie?"

"No. That's her sister, Hester."

Deacon scratched his head. "Seems the wrong Wexler sister showed up to check on you."

"Yeah. Weird. Hallie must be busy doing something. The cheerleaders have a booth. That's probably where she is. I bet she didn't even see my ride."

"Right. I'm sure that's what it is."

Tanner frowned. "I don't know why Hester came. She doesn't even like me."

"She has a funny way of showing it."

Tanner nodded and Deacon realized his brother had no idea Hester was infatuated with him. He folded his arms across his chest. He loved how innocent his little brother still was.

"You know she likes you, right?"

Tanner looked astounded at the thought. "No way. She's hated me since third grade."

"What happened in third grade?"

"I kind of pushed her off the slide." At Deacon's raised eyebrows, he went on. "Not on purpose. It was an accident. But she swore I meant to do it."

"Hmm. I think she's over it now."

Dr. Hart came into the room, which didn't give Tanner a chance to respond. Dr. Hart had been Connelly's doctor for forty-seven years. He'd delivered all the Carmichael siblings, along with most everyone else in town born during his tenure. He was well-loved and everyone would be sad to see him go when he retired.

Dr. Hart was also aware of Faith's dislike of her children riding horses for anything other than ranch duties. So when he saw a dusty Tanner sitting on his table, he frowned.

"What do we have here, young Carmichael?"

"I rode my first bronc today."

The doctor glanced at Deacon. "And what are you going to tell your mother?"

Deacon shrugged. "I'll think of something."

"How's she doing?"

"She has good days and bad days. She was her old self at the gala though."

"Tell her I want to see her soon."

"I'll try."

Dr. Hart examined Tanner's ankle, as well as giving him a total once over, since he'd taken such a bad fall. X-rays revealed a hairline fracture. That, along with a slight concussion, would keep Tanner off of a horse for a while.

The doctor studied Tanner for a moment after handing him a prescription for a mild pain reliever. "I mean it. No driving for two weeks, and no horses for at least three weeks."

Deacon smiled. "That's like telling him not to eat for three weeks."

"Even so. I want you to get past that concussion. Then once you feel your ankle is up to it, take it slow."

Tanner nodded. "Yes, sir."

Deacon shook hands with Dr. Hart. "I'll keep him tied down for a few weeks."

"Okay. Come see me next week for a follow-up. I'll send you home with crutches. But for the next few days, I want you to stay off of your feet. I'll write you a note for school."

Tanner frowned. "How much school do I have to miss?"

Deacon laughed. "This is the only kid I know of who hates missing school."

Dr. Hart smiled. "At least until Wednesday. See how you feel then."

Tanner nodded. "Okay."

Deacon and Tanner left the clinic and got into the Cherokee.

Deacon glanced at him. "When you were younger, I'd take you for ice cream after a visit to the clinic."

Tanner grinned. "I'll never be too old for ice cream."

Deacon started the engine. "I don't suppose you will. I'm rather fond of it myself still. The café or soft serve from the bakery?"

"The café. I think this calls for a chocolate sundae."

Chapter Twelve

"Okay. I'll remember that if I'm ever questioned."

W hen Tobias told Cassidy to meet him at the second booth from the end at the chili cook-off, she didn't expect to find Deacon manning it with a middle-aged woman. It took a moment for him to spot her. When he did, he motioned for her to come to the front of the line.

She glanced at the people in line. "I'm not cutting. I just need to ask a question." She went to a second window and Deacon opened it.

She smiled at him. "What are you doing?"

"Serving chili."

"I realize that. But why?"

He motioned toward the woman with his head. "That's Ruthie. She makes the best chili in the county. Maybe even the state. I've been helping her every year since I was fifteen."

"Okay." She looked at the line. "I don't want to keep you. Have you seen Tobias?"

"Oh, right. Tobias. He had to take a ride out with some of the men. Had a bit of a coyote problem last night."

"Oh. Okay. I was supposed to meet him here for some chili."

"I'll get you a bowl. He'll show up at some point."

"No. That's okay. I'll wait for him." She looked at the line again. "You better get back to work before they riot."

He smiled. "Yeah. I'll see you around."

She nodded. But before she could leave, he returned to the window. "I don't suppose you'd like to give me a hand? Just until we get this line knocked down?"

"Sure." Much better than waiting around for Tobias to show.

"Come around the back. I'll let you in."

Cassidy circled the booth and found Deacon waiting at the door. He was dressed more casually than she'd seen him yet, in jeans and a t-shirt with Chili Champ 2020 on it.

"They're getting rowdy."

"Uh oh. What do you want me to do?"

"Are you good with money?"

"I can count change." She entered the small space and smiled at Ruthie, who was stirring a large pot of chili on a gas stove.

Ruthie glanced at her and returned her smile. "No time for formal introductions. Grab an apron."

Deacon laughed. "Take the second window. Get their order, call out what it is, then take the money."

"Got it. Do you have a price list?"

"Five dollars for a bowl of chili. If they want a basket of bread or crackers, two dollars more."

"Okay. Easy enough."

Cassidy got to work and after thirty minutes she glanced at Deacon, who was at the other window. He seemed to know everyone who came to his window, and called most of them by name.

She reached over and nudged him. "The line isn't going down."

"I told you, this is the best chili in the county." He glanced down at his shirt. "I have the t-shirt to prove it."

"Will you save me a bowl?"

He smiled at the customer in front of the window. "I'll be right back."

He took Cassidy's arm and brought her to the stove, then retrieved a spoon and dipped out some chili. He held it up, and she leaned in and blew on it, before taking the bite.

She raised her eyebrows. "Wow."

"Good?"

"Spicy."

"But good?"

She nodded. "Really good."

"Okay. Get back to work. Ruthie will save a couple of bowls for us. We'll be sold out in an hour."

Cassidy took countless orders and worked closely with Ruthie and Deacon in the tiny space. She was nudged, bumped into, and moved politely out of the way. But it was all in fun, and she laughed through most of the next hour. She also didn't mind at all being so close to Deacon.

When Ruthie told Deacon they were down to their last ten bowls, excluding the two she was holding back for them, he returned to his window and called out.

"Sorry folks. Only ten more bowls left." He pointed to a man in a dark green jacket. "Tim, you'll be the last customer."

Everyone behind Tim wondered off, mumbling. But they weren't upset. It seemed like it happened every year and they were expecting it at some point.

When the last customer was served, Ruthie sighed loudly.

"Dear sweet Jesus. My feet are killing me."

Deacon put his hands on her shoulders. "Ruthie, go home and put your feet up. You served half of Connelly tonight. I'll clean up."

"Are you sure, sweetheart?"

"Of course. Go."

She kissed him on the cheek. "You don't need to tell me twice."

She took off her apron and smiled at Cassidy. "Thank you, young lady. You were a great help."

"You're welcome. I had fun."

Deacon handed Ruthie the cash box. "Take this home with you. I'll take it to the church for you tomorrow."

"Thank you."

She left and Cassidy looked at Deacon. "The church?"

"All the proceeds go to your favorite charity. Ruthie's is her church. They're saving to repave the parking lot."

"Tonight will certainly help with that."

He turned a milk crate over for her. "Have a seat. I'll get you some chili."

"Thank you."

She sat and watched Deacon at the stove. He kept surprising her. He wasn't nearly the person she thought she met the other night. She was glad she attended the gala and then continued to spend the rest of the weekend with the Carmichaels.

He handed her a bowl of chili and a spoon, then sat on another crate with his own bowl. They were squeezed between the counter and the stove and their knees were almost touching.

He smiled. "Pretty cozy in here." They shared a basket of bread while they ate chili. Halfway through his bowl, he pointed at her. "You're probably thirsty."

"A little. It's pretty spicy."

He opened the small refrigerator and pulled out two bottles of water, then handed her one.

"Oh. Thank you." She took a sip. "Mmm. I think you were right. This has to be the best chili in the county. Possibly in Texas. But I haven't had a chance to taste all the chili in Texas yet."

"You don't need to now."

When someone tapped on the window, Deacon stood, then glanced at Cassidy.

He set his bowl down and went to the window. "It's Tobias." He talked through the glass to Tobias. "Cassidy's in here. Come on around."

Deacon opened the back door, and a few moments later, Tobias stuck his head in.

"Hey."

She held up her chili bowl. "Just a few more bites."

"Take your time. Sorry I'm late."

"It's fine."

"She's been helping Ruthie and me here in the booth. Made my job a lot easier."

"Yeah. I bet. Any chili left?"

"We ate the last of it."

"Dammit. I'll go get a bowl across the way."

Cassidy waved at him. "I'll be right out."

She ate her last bite, then stood as Deacon moved toward her. She ran into him and he stood inches away from her for a moment before taking a step back.

"Whoops. Sorry."

She smiled. "Totally my fault." She avoided looking into his eyes, half afraid of what she might see there.

He stepped out of her way. "Thanks for all your help."

"Of course. I had fun." She looked at the dirty dishes and general disarray of the place.

"Do you need help cleaning up?"

"No. I got it. Go have fun with Tobias."

"Okay. I'll see you later." She ventured a look at his eyes and saw a warmth she hadn't seen before. She headed for the door, not exactly sure what it meant.

She went around the trailer and found Tobias headed toward her with a bowl of chili. They sat at a table and he took a bite of chili then ripped off a piece of bread and put it in his mouth.

"I'm starving."

"Deacon said you were looking for a coyote or something."

He nodded. "A pack of them. Found them on a bluff above the south pasture."

She rested her elbows on the table. "If you spent the last couple of hours killing coyotes, I don't want to hear about it."

"You know how destructive they are, right?"

"Yes. But still."

"Okay. I spent the last few hours not killing coyotes. I brought them treats and taught them a few tricks."

She shook her head. "Fine. I get it."

"They took out three of our cows last night."

"I'm sorry. Poor cows."

"You haven't spent much time around a working ranch, have you?"

"No. Grandpa only raises horses. No cows. No coyote problems."

"They'll take a horse out too if they get a chance. It has to be isolated and not be a stallion, though."

"Can we talk about something other than coyotes eating livestock?"

"Sure." He took a bite of chili.

"How's Tanner doing?"

"Good, considering. He's got a pretty good headache. And he'll be on crutches for a few weeks. No riding for a while. Which is the worst of it, of course."

"What did you tell your mother?"

"I let Deacon do all the lying to our mother. He told her Tanner was helping out at the rodeo and a steer stepped on him."

"Okay. I'll remember that if I'm ever questioned."

Tobias grinned. "The Carmichael dynamics are complicated." He finished his chili, then leaned toward Cassidy and took her hand. "So, I was hoping we might go find somewhere more appropriate for me to give you that kiss I was trying to give you earlier."

Cassidy smiled. "As nice as that sounds, I think I need to call it a night. This has been a crazy weekend and I have to teach school in the morning."

"Right. School teacher. I almost forgot."

"But, I'll take a rain check. Next weekend."

He pointed at her. "Trail ride?"

"Perfect."

Deacon finished up in the booth, then locked up and went around to the front of it. He spotted Cassidy and Tobias having a conversation, and he didn't want to bother them. Actually, he did want to bother them. But he didn't. He slipped away unnoticed and went to his Jeep.

It'd been a really long time since he had fun. But this weekend had been just that. He had a really good time. He sat in the Jeep for a moment and thought about all the times Cassidy smiled at him.

He started the motor. There was no sense going down that road. Cassidy was with Tobias. Or she would be soon. Tobias would treat her well. And maybe being in an actual relationship would prompt him to lay off the rum.

If he didn't, then Deacon would kick his ass. Cassidy deserved better than that.

Chapter Thirteen

"Don't call me bro."

D eacon awoke from a deep sleep and realized he'd been dreaming about Cassidy again. He sighed and got up to get a glass of water. He'd never had dreams about women before, and he wasn't sure what it meant. Or at least he wasn't ready to admit to himself what it meant. It'd been three days since the chili cook-off and he'd dreamt about her every night since. They weren't erotic dreams, but they weren't PG rated, either.

He needed to steer clear of Cassidy O'Hare. It was the only solution.

It took him a while to fall back asleep, so when he woke later in the morning than usual, he was mad at himself. He had some work to do in his office this morning. And he and Tobias were working with some new horses this afternoon. It'd be a full day, and he was getting a late start.

He came downstairs, to find his mother waiting for him at the bottom of the stairs.

"Good morning, Mother."

"Are you okay?"

"Yes, I overslept." She looked at him like he said he'd gone out last night, gotten wasted, and brought a hooker home with him. She was agitated. He took her hand. "What's wrong, Mother? Did you need something?"

"Tanner's schoolwork. I don't want him to get behind."

"He's only missed two days. And he'll probably go back tomorrow. He's an A student. He'll be fine."

"I want you to go talk to his teachers."

"I've got a crazy day today."

"What's more important than your brother's education?"

When his mother got a bee in her bonnet, she wouldn't let it go. "Fine. I'll go this afternoon. Or maybe Tobias could go."

"I want you to go."

He patted her hand. "Yes, Mother."

He headed for his office and she called after him. "You need to eat breakfast, dear."

Like he had time for that now. "Can you ask Ruthie to bring me something? I need to make some phone calls."

"Of course, dear."

During his second call, which was long distance to a horse dealer in Florida, Ruthie came in with a tray for him. She set it on the desk as he ended the call.

"Thank you."

She nodded. "Your mother's a bit on edge today."

"I noticed."

"She's wandering around the house like she doesn't know what to do with herself."

"It's because Tanner's home. Her schedule is off. Ask Tanner to read to her. That might calm her down."

"Good idea. I'll ask him."

"Thanks, Ruthie."

"You eat now, before it gets cold."

"Yes, ma'am."

Deacon figured his best bet would be to hit the school during lunch break and pick up Tanner's homework. So he called the school office and asked them if they could have it ready for him. He spent another two hours catching up on work. The big weekend had put him behind. He didn't like being behind. So by the time he headed for the school, he wasn't in the best mood.

He parked in the bus loading area, which wasn't quite legal, but he figured the buses wouldn't be there for another three hours. He entered the office and had to wait behind two other parents who were there for disciplinary reasons. It reminded him of Tobias' high school days. After their father died, Tobias went through a rebellious stage as a way of coping with the loss, and Deacon had tried to be patient with him. But he'd spent many afternoons talking to the principal.

When he reached the head of the line, the secretary greeted him warmly. "Good afternoon, Mr. Carmichael."

"Hi. I called earlier about Tanner's homework."

"Yes. I have most of it right here." She looked through what she had. "Let's see. History. Biology. Spanish." She looked at Deacon. "Looks like we're missing algebra and English." She looked through the papers again. "Oh. No. Here's the work from Mr. Thomas. So just Miss O'Hare's class."

Deacon took the paperwork from her. "Thank you." He debated on skipping the English homework. But it was Tanner's favorite class. He'd notice if it wasn't there. "So, how do I track down Miss O'Hare?"

"She generally eats in the classroom. Room 113. Straight down the hall. First left. Second door on the right.

"Got it. Thanks."

It'd be fine. In and out. No problem.

He followed the secretary's directions, then tapped on the door of room 113. He peered through the small window and saw Cassidy at her desk eating a sandwich. She was in schoolteacher mode, wearing a pretty blouse, with her hair pulled back into a ponytail. She looked up from her desk and spotted him, then waved him in.

"Hey. What are you doing here?"

Deacon held up the assignments. "Tanner's homework."

"Oh my gosh. I totally forgot."

"It's fine. I'll tell him—"

"No. No. It'll just take me a minute."

Cassidy looked good in her schoolteacher attire, but Deacon tried not to notice. He didn't want to dream about the sexy schoolteacher tonight.

She smiled at him. "How have you been?"

"Busy. As always. Playing catch up after the weekend."

"Right. Sorry. Now I'm keeping you."

She wrote some things on a notepad, folded it, and tucked it into a paperback book, before standing, and coming around the desk.

"I'm still coming down from our exciting weekend."

He nodded. He caught a whiff of something floral. He wasn't sure what it was, but it was distracting. In a good way.

She handed him the book. "He needs to read the first six chapters and answer the questions I wrote down."

"Okay. Is that it?"

"That's it."

He nodded again, then headed for the door.

"Deacon?"

He stopped, thought of a couple curse words, and turned back to her.

"Is everything okay?"

"Yeah. Why wouldn't it be?"

"Just wondering. You seem a little... Sorry. Say hi to Tanner for me."

"I will."

------- ❧ -------

When the door closed behind Deacon, Cassidy returned to her desk. What was that all about? It was like he'd never met her before. She tried to shake it off. Maybe her first impression of him was right. Or maybe there was something going on with the Carmichaels. She wanted there to be an excuse for his abruptness. She picked up her phone and dialed Tobias.

It took a few rings before he answered. "Hey, schoolteacher."

"Tobias."

"Shouldn't you be enriching young minds right now?"

"It's lunch break."

"Oh, okay. So, have you missed me?"

She smiled. "Yes. I have."

"Are we still on for Saturday?"

"Definitely."

"Awesome."

"I wanted to make sure everything was okay at your place."

"As far as I know. Why? Have you heard something? Has something happened I don't know about?"

"No. I'm sure everything's fine. Deacon was here to pick up Tanner's homework, and he seemed a little testy."

"That's just Deacon. He's back to captain of the ship mode."

"That must be it."

"Plus, our mother insisted he go pick up Tanner's work, even though he's going back to school tomorrow. Which probably pissed Deacon off. But she's in one of her moods today. He likes to keep her appeased so it doesn't escalate. But he doesn't always like it."

"Okay. That explains it. I'm sorry to bother you."

"You never bother me. Call me anytime. I'll see you on Saturday, early afternoon."

"I'll be there."

When Deacon showed up at the training pen, Tobias could tell he was still in the foul mood he'd been in when Cassidy saw him.

Tobias smiled. "What's up, bro?"

"Don't call me bro." He picked up a long lead rope and entered the pen. The horse in the middle of it eyed him warily. He was a half-broke, newly gelded thoroughbred, who'd been giving them fits for a few days.

Tobias climbed onto the fence and sat on the top rail. "I think he's pissed we took away his manhood."

"I don't blame him." Deacon approached the horse, who snorted, then trotted away. Deacon kept moving toward him. "Come on, boy. There's nowhere to go."

Feeling trapped, the horse hopped back and forth for a minute, then veered away and circled the edge of the pen, running right past Tobias.

Tobias swore and turned to the side to avoid being hit. "I think he did that on purpose."

Deacon moved toward the horse again. The horse watched him approach, and this time held his ground. Deacon stopped five feet away. "I'm not going to hurt you."

The horse veered away again.

"Damn stubborn horse."

Tobias laughed. "I think it's kind of a draw."

Deacon let the horse circle the pen. When he stopped moving, Deacon walked toward him again. This time, the horse let him get closer. Deacon reached a hand out. "I just want to give you a pet." The horse stared at him, but didn't move away. Deacon took another step. He was close enough now to touch the halter, but he waited. The horse blinked a few times, then whinnied. Deacon reached for the halter and the horse remained still. "There you go." He stroked the horse's neck. "See now, what was all the fuss about?"

He connected the lead to the halter, then stroked the horse's nose. "You like that, don't you?" Working with horses, no matter how stubborn they were, calmed Deacon down. The first few years after his father's death, he spent a lot of time in the barn or the training pen with horses. It was what got him through.

The horse nodded, and Tobias laughed. "You got him."

Deacon glance at Tobias. "Horses, I can win over. People not so much."

"You just don't try hard enough. Although you were damn near human over the weekend. You had Cassidy believing you were a nice guy."

Deacon released three feet on the lead, then coaxed the horse to move, before walking him around the pen. "Be sure to set her straight on that."

"I think you already did."

Deacon stopped in front of Tobias. "What do you mean?"

"She called me after you left the school. She was worried something was wrong."

"She called?"

"Yeah. Seems you wore your grumpy pants to school."

Deacon sighed and started walking again. "I wasn't grumpy. I was in a hurry."

"I see. It was probably just her imagination."

"Yeah."

"She was expecting the guy she shared a bowl of chili with."

Deacon looked at Tobias. "What's wrong with sharing a bowl of chili?"

"Nothing."

"Come take over. I'm going to go get a longer rope. I want to run him a little."

Tobias jumped to the ground and took the lead from Deacon. "You're way uptight, man."

"I'm not uptight."

Tobias nodded. "You need to get yourself laid. That's your problem."

"How do you know I'm not getting laid somewhere?"

"Because you're home every night and in your room by ten."

"Maybe I sneak women into my room after everyone's in bed."

Tobias shook his head, then pointed at him. "No. That's me. Of course not now that I'm in love. You've never done anything scandalous in your life."

"I've been scandalous."

"Not in the last ten years."

"Keep him moving. I'll be right back."

Chapter Fourteen

"Thank you, Dr. Carmichael."

Deacon was in the middle of a fairly explicit dream about Cassidy when a knock on his door woke him. He tried to clear his head. "Go away."

Tobias opened the door. "Good morning, sunshine."

"Did you not hear the go away part?"

Tobias sat on a chair next to the bed and put his feet on the blankets. Deacon frowned at Tobias' boots. "Get your feet off my bed."

Tobias dropped his feet to the ground. "I need some advice."

Deacon rolled onto his back. "My office hours don't start until nine."

"Where can I take Cassidy on a horse that will be...romantic?"

Deacon stuck an extra pillow behind his head and sighed. "Well, the horseback ride itself can be romantic."

"True. But I'm thinking a picnic lunch. You must know a spot. Back before you became a robot, you took your share of horseback rides with a young lady or two."

"When you're soliciting advice, flattery is probably a better choice than mockery."

"Sorry. So, what do you have?"

Deacon thought for a moment. "Angel Falls."

"Yeah. I guess. Seems kind of cliché."

"Not in front of it. If you climb the rocks on the left side, there's an opening that'll take you behind the waterfall."

"Really? How come I don't know about that?"

"Dad showed it to me. It was kind of our secret spot. I haven't been back since... Anyway. It might be romantic with the right company."

"Thanks. That's where I'll take her." He stood.

Deacon looked at him. "You really like this one, don't you?"

Tobias grinned. "Isn't it obvious?" He left the room and Deacon rolled onto his side.

"Of course you finally fall for the one woman, who I'd..." He put the pillow over his head. *You have a plan. And that plan doesn't include Cassidy or any other woman.* "Your plan sucks, man."

Deacon walked into the barn and found Cassidy saddling Nutmeg. Standing next to her, Tobias' horse Chance was already saddled.

"What are you doing here?"

Cassidy looked at him, then resumed tightening the cinch. "You always have such a warm greeting for me." She glanced at him again. "I'm going on a trail ride with Tobias."

Deacon thought about the conversation he had with Tobias that morning. Finding Cassidy getting ready to take a romantic trail ride with Tobias made him irrationally angry, which usually didn't work out so well for him. But even so, it never seemed to stop him.

"Why are you leading him on?"

She pulled the cinch tight and buckled it, then turned to him. "Excuse me?"

"If you're not interested in him, then you shouldn't be going on a date with him."

She cocked her head. "Who says this is a date? And what business is it of yours?"

"Tobias considers it a date. And you accepting the invitation is a green light."

She turned back to the horse and gave the saddle a tug, then glanced over her shoulder at him. "Why do you care?"

"Because, for the first time in his life, I believe Tobias has actual feelings for you. And if you're playing him, then it's definitely my business."

"What makes you think I'm playing him?"

Deacon took a step toward her. "Because even though you don't want to admit it to yourself, you're interested in a different Carmichael brother."

"Wow."

"You know it's true."

"You mean Mr. Unavailable? Mr.—"

He took her arm. "Don't use Tobias to get to me."

"I have no interest in you, Deacon." She tried to pull her arm away, but he held tight.

He leaned in close to her and she slapped his face. He released her arm and took a step back as he put a hand on his face. Cassidy mounted

Nutmeg and nearly ran him over on her way out of the barn. Tobias was coming through the door and jumped out of the way.

He looked at Deacon. "What's going on?" He walked over to him. "What'd you say to her?"

Deacon sighed, then shook his head. "Just living up to my name."

"Bastard?"

"I was thinking, asshole. But bastard works too."

Tobias took Chance's halter. "I need to go after her."

"I'll go. It's my mess. I'll clean it up." He mounted Chance.

Tobias looked at him. "You still didn't tell me what you said to her."

"You don't want to know." He trotted out of the barn, then once he cleared the yard, he broke into a gallop.

Deacon raced after Cassidy. She had a bit of a head start, so it took him a few minutes to gain on her. He had her in sight when she continued through a creek at a full gallop. She lost control halfway through and Nutmeg stumbled. Cassidy and the horse both went down into the water.

Deacon pulled up short of the water and jumped off Chance. He waded past Cassidy, who was struggling to her feet, and went to the horse. Nutmeg had gotten to his feet and was shaking off the water. He whinnied and held up his right front foot.

Deacon glared at Cassidy. "Dammit. You can't run full bore into a creek not knowing what you're crossing over." He tried to calm the horse, then checked his leg. "Shit." He looked at Cassidy again. "It's one thing to be pissed at me. It's quite another to lose your head and abuse your horse."

She was still standing knee-deep in the water. "Is he hurt?"

Deacon didn't answer as he took Nutmeg's reins and coaxed him back to shore. The horse followed him, but was reluctant to walk on his injured leg. Once on shore, Deacon knelt and checked the leg again.

Cassidy came up behind him. "I didn't mean to hurt him. I'd never—"

"Well, you did." Deacon stood. "I don't think it's too serious. But you can't ride him back."

"How far back is it?"

Deacon looked around to get his bearings. "About two miles."

"Okay. I'll lead him back."

Deacon sighed. "You're not walking back. We'll double up on Chance." He noticed she was holding her left wrist. "Are you hurt?"

She dropped her arms to her sides. "No."

"Let me see it."

She hesitated before holding out her left hand. He took it in his and examined her wrist. "Looks like a sprain."

"Thank you, Dr. Carmichael."

"Seeing as I'm willing to share my ride back with you. You should probably be a little nicer to me."

She looked at him for a moment, then went to Nutmeg, and laid her head against his neck.

Deacon gave her a moment, then took Nutmeg's reins and tied them to his saddle. He mounted Chance, and held a hand out to Cassidy. She put her foot in the stirrup and got up behind Deacon.

"I know you're mad at me. But you should probably hold on."

She put her hands on his side and held onto his jacket as he started Chance walking. He glanced back to see how Nutmeg was moving. The horse seemed to be getting past the initial pain. He was favoring the leg, but not resisting the lead.

They were halfway back before Deacon cleared his throat and spoke. "You're getting me wet."

"You're the one who told me to hang on."

"So I did." He was quiet for another minute, then said, "I'm sorry. I was reacting to something else, and I took it out on you."

"An apology? That's unexpected."

"I have no problem admitting when I'm wrong."

"Good, because you're definitely wrong. I have no interest in you."

"That's good. Because I have no interest in you, either."

"You've made it quite clear you don't want or need a woman in your life. I'd be an idiot to pursue a dead-end."

"And you're not an idiot." He was quiet for a few more minutes, then asked, "How's your arm?"

"It's fine."

He poked it and she pulled it away. "Ouch!"

"Don't lie to me."

"I told you at the gala, I always tell the truth."

"Hmm." They went up an incline. "Hold on. I don't want to have to stop and pick your ass up off the ground."

"Even though it might get you wet?"

"Yes. Even so."

She tightened her grip on his jacket. "I'm not playing Tobias. I like him. He's sweet and fun to be around."

"Yeah. He's a riot."

"I'm not in love with him or anything."

"Of course. That'd be premature. You just met him."

The ranch came into view and Deacon could see Tobias outside the barn.

"I promise you, I won't hurt him."

"That's all I can ask."

Deacon rode up to Tobias, who helped Cassidy off Chase, then he went to Nutmeg.

"What happened?"

Deacon started to say something, but Cassidy spoke first.

"It's my fault. I tried to cross the creek too fast. It was careless, and I'm really sorry."

Deacon dismounted and tied Chance to a post, then joined Tobias next to Nutmeg.

"I think it's a stone bruise. He should be fine in a few days. Wouldn't hurt to have Dr. Benton come take a look, though."

Tobias looked at Deacon and then Cassidy. "Is one of you going to tell me what's going on?"

Deacon patted Nutmeg on the rump. "I'll let Cassidy explain." He nodded at Cassidy, then headed for the house.

Tobias looked at Cassidy. "Well?"

She went to sit on a bale of hay. "It was a misunderstanding, and I overreacted."

"By misunderstanding, you mean Deacon was being a prick."

"Yeah. I guess. It was my fault too. It's fine. I really don't want to talk about it."

He smiled at her. "You've already had your horseback ride. Maybe we should take our picnic lunch to the pond instead. It's a nice walk."

She nodded. "That sounds good." She held up her arm. "I don't suppose you have an ace bandage lying around?"

He knelt in front of her and looked at her wrist. "It's a bit swollen. Do you want me to take you into the clinic?"

"No. I'll just wrap it."

He stood and took her right hand. "Come on. We have a magical cupboard in here with anything you could ever want for human and animal injuries."

He led her into a side room off the barn. It was an office of sorts, with a desk and three chairs. But there was also a small kitchen area with a coffeemaker, a microwave, and a sink. In the corner, there was a refrigerator, and Tobias pulled out a tray of ice. He put some cubes into a plastic bag and handed it to her.

"Put this on it."

She put the ice on her wrist and sat in one of the chairs, while Tobias dug through a drawer for an ace bandage. He brought it to her, knelt, then wrapped her wrist.

She looked at him. "Thank you."

"Got to take care of my girl."

Deacon appeared in the doorway and Cassidy set her hand in her lap, as Tobias stood.

"I called Dr. Benton. He'll come by in an hour or so."

"Oh. Good. Are you going to be around? We were going to walk up to the pond."

"Sure. I got it. Go have your picnic."

"Thanks, man."

Cassidy stood and Deacon nodded toward her wrist.

"He got you fixed up there, I see."

"Yes. It's feeling much better."

"Good." He backed up a step. "Have fun."

"Thank you."

Chapter Fifteen

"Are you psychoanalyzing me?"

Cassidy and Tobias took their picnic lunch and walked the half-mile to the pond. It was created by their grandfather and filled with water from one of the year-round creeks on the property. The water was diverted to the pond, then released on the other side back into the creek. It was big enough to row a boat on. And it was stocked with trout.

They sat at a table on the wooden dock stretching twenty feet over the water. As Cassidy set their lunch out, Tobias watched her.

"I'd sure like to know what transpired between you and Deacon."

"Really, I don't want to talk about it. He apologized. That's all that matters. And I'm the one who took off and hurt Nutmeg. I should be the one apologizing to both of you. And to Nutmeg." She looked at him. "He's going to be okay, right?"

"Yes. He'll be fine."

"Can we not talk about it anymore?"

"Sure." He picked up his sandwich. "I should've brought the fishing poles."

She smiled. "I haven't fished since I was in high school."

"Are you any good?"

"I'm not bad. I'm sure you're much better."

"I'm a little too impatient. I tend to cast, reel in. Cast, reel in. Deacon, as you can imagine, is a good fisherman. The man with the patience of Job."

"I can see that."

"He's been super wound up since the weekend. I need to get him out here to relax. I told him to get laid, but that's probably not going to happen anytime soon."

Cassidy nodded. "He is a bit uptight."

"Fishing should help." He grinned. "I mean, it's not the same as getting laid, but it'll have to do. It's not like I can go out and get him a girl."

"That is something I'm sure he'd want to take care of himself."

He reached across the table and took her hand. "Speaking of getting laid—"

"Tobias!"

"No. That totally came out wrong. Whoa. Sorry." He laughed. "What I meant to say is maybe after we eat, we could...make out a little."

Cassidy smiled. "Tobias. You're pretty cute."

"I am, aren't I?"

"Let's finish these sandwiches then we'll talk about it."

He squeezed her hand. "You make me feel like I'm in high school again."

"That's a little weird for me since I teach high school."

"Right. But then there's the whole sexy school teacher..."

"Ew. No."

He laughed. "Sorry. Just a thought."

"All of a sudden, you're not so cute anymore."

"I'm sorry. I'll shut up and eat my sandwich."

"Excellent idea."

Cassidy and Tobias had a very nice afternoon together. They cuddled and kissed, and Tobias mostly behaved himself. Cassidy didn't think of Deacon the whole time they were at the pond. But on the walk back, her mind returned to their conversation on the horse. What was that all about?

She took Tobias' hand. "Thank you for a great afternoon."

"Thank you for making it great."

"So, what's your week look like?"

"Monday, Deacon and I need to drive to East Fork and deliver a couple of horses. And on Wednesday afternoon, we need to go look at a bull."

"Don't you have a bull?"

"We have two. But we like to mix it up once in a while. The herds are a little bigger this year. We don't want to tire them out, if you know what I mean."

"Yes. I know what you mean. So what time of year do they... you know?"

"Breed?" He laughed. "We start in February and go through March."

"And when do they deliver?"

"November through January."

"So you'll have a bunch of baby cows soon?"

"Yes. In a couple months."

"That should be fun."

"It's not fun. It's a lot of work. We hire extra men for those six months. Otherwise Deacon, Tanner, and I'd be overrun."

"I love that you guys are so hands-on. But you could sit back and—"

"Count our money?"

"Something like that."

"Our great-grandfather, our grandfather, and our father worked the cattle alongside the hands their whole lives. Just because it's now a pretty impressive empire, doesn't mean we're going to sit back and live sweet off the labor of our forefathers."

She stopped walking and looked at him. "And that, right there, is why you have an impressive empire. You don't take it for granted. You're not afraid or too good to get your hands dirty."

"It's how we were raised. We may be the hoity-toity Carmichaels at Mother's gala. But the rest of the year, we're just cowboys."

"Hoity-toity?"

"You know what I mean. It's a word, right?"

She put her arm around his waist. "Yes, Yale man. You really did party your way through school, didn't you?"

"I was kind of forced into going, like Abby. I didn't really see the point. I'd just come back and be a cowboy. I didn't need a degree from Yale to do that."

"Maybe. But you use words like hoity-toity now, so it was obviously four years well spent."

───────────── ❈ ─────────────

Abby came into the barn after working with her horse for a couple of hours. Deacon was there mucking out a stall. She put her horse away, then picked up a rake and went in to help him.

She glanced at him. "Must be serious."

"What do you mean?"

"You hate mucking stalls. It's the one job you'll always pass on to someone else. Unless..."

"Unless what?"

"Unless you're either really pissed off about something or you're in pain. Emotionally, not physically."

He leaned on the shovel handle and looked at her. "When I was a kid, I was pretty even tempered." He smiled. "Probably hard for you to imagine that. But I was. However, once in a while, some kid at school would piss me off. Or some girl would break my heart. And Dad would hand me a shovel. He'd say nothing clears a man's head like shoveling shit."

Abby laughed. "I miss Dad."

"Do you even remember him?"

"I remember he was big. And strong. And he always had a smile on his face."

Deacon nodded. "That describes him perfectly."

"I wish I had spent as much time with him as you did."

"I'm thankful every day for that."

"So, which is it today?"

"Hmm?"

"Are you pissed at someone, or did some girl break your heart?"

Deacon started shoveling again. "Both."

Abby put her rake down, then put her arms around Deacon's neck. She hugged him for several moments.

When she stepped away, he smiled at her. "What was that for?"

"Shoveling shit isn't always enough. Sometimes, you need a hug, too."

Deacon finished cleaning the stall and had moved to another when Tobias and Cassidy came into the barn. Tobias leaned against the gate.

"I knew something was up with you."

Deacon glanced at him, then nodded to Cassidy, who was beside him. "Just cleaning stalls." He scooped up a pile of used hay and dumped it into a plastic garbage can.

Tobias looked at Cassidy. "Deacon will do most any job on this ranch. But cleaning stalls isn't one of them. Who are you pissed at, man?"

"I'm about to get pissed at you if you don't go away and leave me to it."

"Fine. Muck away." Tobias went to check on Nutmeg, but Cassidy stayed at the stall.

Deacon glanced at her, then picked up another shovelful of hay. "How's the wrist?"

"It's fine. Doesn't hurt anymore."

"How was the pond?"

"It was nice. Tobias wished he'd brought some fishing gear."

"He sucks at fishing." He switched out his shovel for a rake to get the last remnants of hay.

Cassidy laughed. "That's what he said. He said you were good, though."

"I can catch a fish if I want to, yeah."

"Can you stop that for a moment?"

Deacon stopped and leaned the rake against the wall. He glanced at Tobias.

"I think we've said everything that needs to be said."

"I just want to know where that came from earlier. On Sunday night, we parted friends. Now it seems you're mad at me. But I don't know what I did. Prior to hurting Nutmeg, that is."

"I'm not mad at you. I'm mad at me."

"Why?"

Deacon shrugged. "Because I'm an asshole."

"I don't believe that."

"You saw it firsthand just a little while ago."

"I also spent most of the weekend with you. Asshole is your go-to when you're feeling vulnerable."

He pulled off his gloves. "Are you psychoanalyzing me?"

"I'm telling you what I see."

Tobias returned. "What did Dr. Benton say?"

Deacon left the stall and closed the gate behind him. "A stone bruise like we thought. He iced him for thirty minutes and said to do it again tonight if Nutmeg is still favoring it."

"So it's not too bad?"

"No. He should be better in a day or two."

Cassidy put a hand to her heart. "Oh. Thank goodness."

Deacon glanced at her. "We got lucky."

Tobias frowned at him. "Come on, man. She feels bad enough."

"Right. Sorry. I'm going to go get cleaned up for dinner. Mother's in a bit of a mood still. So tread softly."

"Okay. I'll be in soon."

Tobias watched him go, then turned to Cassidy. "Sorry. He says Mother's in a mood. I'm pretty sure her moods coincide with his."

"It's fine. Why'd you assume he was mad about something when you saw him in the stall?"

"It was our dad's cure-all for testy young men. Go muck out a stall and clear your head.

"Does it work?"

"It did for the troubles of a teenager. Not sure it works for whatever is ailing him."

"Grown up troubles do often require more than a shovel and a pile of crap."

Tobias put his arm around her. "From the mouth of babes. And by babes, I don't mean tiny humans."

"I'm pretty sure I know what you mean."

Chapter Sixteen

"This ranch life is starting to grow on me."

When his phone rang and woke him, Deacon considered not answering it. He tried to think if it could be any of his siblings. As far as he knew, they were all safe in bed. He picked up the phone and didn't recognize the number.

"What the hell. Hello?"

"Deacon."

He sat up. "Cassidy?"

"Yes. I'm so sorry to bother you. I assume I woke you."

"Yeah. It's fine. Why are you calling? I didn't even know you had my number."

"Tobias gave it to me in case I couldn't get a hold of him. He said you usually knew where he was."

"So, you're calling for Tobias?"

"Yes. Sorry. He's not answering his phone."

Deacon looked at the time. "Could be because it's midnight." He remembered Tobias was having a bad night and had drank a little too much. "What do you need? I think Tobias is out for the night."

"Oh. It's fine. I'll figure it out."

Deacon rubbed his face. "Cassidy. Just tell me what's going on."

"It's Queenie."

"Queenie?"

"Grandpa's mare who is in foal. I think she's in labor."

"Where's Winston?"

"He's gone for the weekend. I'm here alone. The mare was making such a racket, I came to see what was wrong and... I don't know what to do. I've never delivered a horse before."

Deacon could tell she was on the verge of panicking. "Are you with her now?"

"Yes. She quieted down when she saw me."

"Okay. Give me twenty minutes. I'll come over and check her out."

"I don't want you to do that. It's fine. I'll call Dr. Benton."

Dr. Benton was on an emergency call on the other side of the county. A horse trailer with six horses went off the road and flipped. Last Deacon heard, at least three of the horses didn't make it.

"I'm pretty sure he's gone, too. Just hang tight. I'll be right over."

"Thank you."

He ended the call. Of course he had to go help her, even if it broke his 'steer clear of Cassidy' rule. He got dressed, then left the house.

It took him closer to thirty minutes to get there, and when he entered the barn, Cassidy was in the stall with Queenie. The horse was still on her feet, but it looked like she was getting close to foaling.

Cassidy was relieved to see Deacon. "Oh my goodness. Thank you."

He went into the stall and stroked Queenie, then checked her to make sure everything was progressing as it should, and she was nearing delivery.

"She's close."

"Will she need help?"

Deacon smiled. "They generally do all right on their own." He stepped away from the horse. "But we'll keep watch." He took Cassidy's arm and led her to a bale of hay several feet away. Winston had moved Queenie to the foaling stall before he left. It was larger than the others and had fresh hay and clean water. "Looks like Winston knew she was close."

"He told me she'd deliver soon, but he expected to make it back in time. He'll be home this afternoon."

"I guess Queenie had her own idea about it."

They sat. "How long does it take?"

"Depends on the horse. Is this her first?"

"I think so. I'm not sure." She looked at him. "Thank you for coming. Even if she doesn't need any help. I'm glad you're here."

"No problem. She's close. It won't be long."

They watched Queenie for a few minutes before she asked, "So, you said Tobias was down for the night. Is that code for he's been drinking?"

Deacon sighed. "Yeah. Not too much. But enough to sleep through a phone call." Queenie suddenly laid down, and Cassidy gasped. Deacon took her hand. "It's okay. She's fine. It just means she's getting close."

She glanced at him and kept hold of his hand. Over the next thirty minutes, they watched as Queenie delivered her foal without any help. It was beautiful and when Deacon glanced at Cassidy, he saw she had tears in her eyes. He wiped one away with his thumb.

"Pretty amazing, huh?"

She nodded.

The colt laid still for a few moments, then started to move and free himself from the fetal membranes. Queenie nuzzled him and he seemed to perk up.

Cassidy put her free hand to her mouth. "Oh, my gosh. He's the cutest thing I've ever seen."

Deacon laughed. "I think the first person who sees him gets to name him."

"But you're here, too."

"I've named plenty of horses. This one's yours."

She thought for a few minutes, then finally said, "Precious."

Deacon smiled. "You know, he's going to be a big old male horse in a few years."

"I don't care. He'll always be Precious to me."

"Precious it is."

It took an hour for the colt to struggle to his feet. Shortly after that, he wobbled to his mother and began to nurse.

Cassidy shook her head. "It keeps getting more and more precious."

"Well, he's aptly named then."

"Are they going to be alright now?"

"We'll, keep watch a while longer. As long as Precious keeps eating and Queenie eats and drinks soon, they'll be fine. But we want to make sure that happens."

"Okay." She leaned back against the wall behind them.

Deacon glanced at her. "You can go to bed if you want. I can stay and keep an eye on them."

"No. I want to stay."

"Okay." He leaned back, too. "There's something about being in a barn in the middle of the night with all the horses sleeping."

She nodded. "It's very peaceful." An owl hooted nearby, and she laughed. "I guess Mr. Owl has something to say about that.

She shivered, and he put his arm around her. "It's a little chilly."

She rested her head on his shoulder and closed her eyes. "This ranch life is starting to grow on me."

Deacon smiled as he resisted the urge to kiss her. It helped to have someone to enjoy it with.

Cassidy woke and opened her eyes. It took her a moment to remember where she was. She was curled up on the hay bale with a blanket for a pillow and Deacon's jacket over her. Deacon was standing with Queenie, brushing her down.

Cassidy sat up and stretched. "I fell asleep."

"You sure did. You know you snore, right?"

"I do not."

Deacon laughed. "Okay. I guess you'd know."

She tried to ignore what his laugh did to her. He was sure to change back into grumpy Deacon soon. "How's Queenie and Precious?"

"Both doing fine."

"Did you sleep?"

"A little, yeah."

She stood and went to Queenie's head. She rubbed her nose as she looked at the colt. "Do you suppose she'll let me pet Precious?"

Deacon looked at Queenie and her baby. "As long as you don't get between her and the colt. Stay on the far side of him."

"Okay." She moved carefully toward the colt and knelt in front of him. "You are so beautiful." She glanced up at Deacon, who was watching her. "I love him so much."

He smiled. "He is something. No matter how many times I experience it, it's always a miracle."

"How many births have you seen?"

"Horses? Probably close to fifty. But then there are cows, sheep, goats. Lots of puppies and kittens." He shook his head. "Too many to count. I damn near had to deliver Tanner. I was sixteen and my dad was out of town. Mom went into labor in the middle of the night and I had to drive her into the clinic in Weston because Dr. Hart was away on an emergency. I was sure we weren't going to make it."

"But you did?"

He nodded. "Tanner was born thirty minutes after we arrived."

"Oh my goodness." She left the colt and went back to Queenie. "You did good, girl." She looked at Deacon. "Can I fix you some breakfast?"

"Ah. No. I should go." He set the curry brush down and headed for the gate. "These guys will be fine now. Maybe check on them every few hours. But I don't expect anything's going to happen now. Leave a message with Dr. Benton's service to let him know she delivered. He'll want to come take a look at the both of them."

"Okay. And Grandpa will be home later. He's going to be so sorry he missed it."

Deacon smiled at her. "I'm kind of glad he did."

Cassidy followed him into the main section of the barn. "I can't thank you enough."

"You don't need to thank me."

She moved close to him and gave him a hug. "Yes. I do."

He embraced the hug, then pulled back and looked at her. She met his eyes, and he couldn't resist any longer. He leaned in and kissed her.

He let go of her and stepped back. "Oh shit. I'm sorry."

"It's okay."

"No. It's not." He moved back another few steps. "I don't know where that came from. I should go."

"Deacon, wait."

He took a breath and stopped. She walked to him and put her arms around his neck and returned his kiss. He put his hands on her arms and pulled them from his neck, then held her hands for a moment before letting go.

"I can't. This can't happen." He looked at her for a moment, then turned and walked away.

———————— ❧❦ ————————

As he headed for the door, Deacon was thankful she didn't call after him. He never would've been able to keep going if she had. He made it to his truck and drove away.

Five miles from the ranch, he pulled over and got out of the truck. He slammed the door and cursed to the early morning sky, scaring a flock of birds perched along the electrical wire. He took a few deep breaths, then cursed again, before sitting in the grass on the side of the road and leaning against his truck. He stayed there and watched the sun come up over the bluffs. By the time he left, he'd found some semblance of peace, and he drove home.

When he pulled up to the house, Tobias was on the porch.

"Shit." Deacon got out of the truck and went up the steps.

"Morning. Where have you been? You're not just getting in, are you? I'm pretty sure I remember you going to bed right after reprimanding me and taking away my bottle."

"One of Winston's horses foaled last night. Cassidy called looking for you. When she couldn't get you, she called me."

"Was it Queenie?"

"Yeah. She did fine. Had a colt."

"You went and helped Cassidy?"

"Yeah. Been there since midnight." He didn't want to stand there and converse with Tobias like he hadn't just kissed Cassidy. "I'm going to go catch a few hours of sleep."

Tobias put a hand on his shoulder. "Thanks, man."

Deacon shook his head. "Don't thank me. Just answer your damn phone next time she calls."

He headed into the house and made it to his room without running into anyone else. He kicked off his boots and dropped onto the bed. He hated that he kissed Cassidy. But he also loved it. It was the best damn kiss he'd ever had.

"She's with Tobias."

He closed his eyes. It sure didn't feel like she was with Tobias. She kissed him back. He was leaving, and she kissed him back.

"It doesn't matter. She was confused. And tired. She'd just experienced something miraculous. That's all it was."

He stared at the ceiling. "I'm talking to myself. That can't be good."

He fell asleep, and this time he didn't dream about Cassidy. Maybe because he'd finally experienced the real thing.

Chapter Seventeen

"Wow! And holy moly!"

Cassidy still had Deacon's coat. So she brought it with her when Tobias asked her to come to dinner with the family. She was still confused over how she felt about Deacon. In the moment, she was all in. That kiss was the beginning of something. But now, four days later, she wasn't so sure. His parting words haunted her. Deacon was a proud man. And he was loyal. Even if he had feelings for her, he'd never come between her and Tobias.

But could she keep seeing Tobias, knowing how Deacon felt? Knowing how she thought she felt? She wasn't sure. If that moment in the barn was real, it'd be just as wrong of her to stay in a relationship with Tobias as it would be for Deacon to interfere.

Tonight she'd know. When she saw Deacon and Tobias together, she'd know what to do. She just hoped she could make it through dinner.

When she arrived at the house, she didn't see anyone. But she figured Tobias might be in the barn, so she parked her car and headed that way. When she went inside, she heard someone singing. It wasn't something you hear every day in a barn full of horses. She followed the sound. Whoever it was, he was pretty good. She tried to recognize the song, but it didn't come to her. Definitely country. Probably old country.

It had to be Tobias. She couldn't picture Deacon singing. Whistling maybe on a really good day. But full on singing? No way.

She opened the door to what she assumed was a storeroom or work area. It wasn't. Deacon was standing there, fresh out of the shower, with a towel in his hands. It was conveniently hanging in front of him, so she only saw him in most of his glory, not all of it. But in the moment before she turned away, she saw enough. Muscled chest, strong thighs, and the biceps of a working cowboy.

She shrieked and turned her back to him. "Oh, my God! Deacon!"

"Yep. Were you expecting Tobias?"

"Yes. I mean, no. I heard you singing. I thought it was him. I had no idea there was a shower in here. Or that you sing." She put a hand to her face. "Why is there a shower in the barn?"

"Sometimes we get really dirty and we don't want to track it into the house."

"Of course. Makes perfect sense."

"Do you have any more questions? Or can I get dried off and put my clothes on?"

"I think I'm done, and I'll leave you to do whatever."

"Thank you."

"You're welcome. Or, yeah. I'm going to go now."

She left and closed the door behind her, leaning on it for a moment. *Wow! And holy moly!* She stayed there for several moments, knowing she should move, because once he was dressed, he'd come out that door. Him knocking her to the ground would only add to the embarrassment. But she seemed to be the only one who was embarrassed. He seemed fine with the encounter. When she heard someone coming into the barn, she moved away from the door. Tobias came in and smiled when he saw her.

"Hello there, schoolteacher."

"Hi." She tried to put on her best, I'm cool, everything's cool, look.

He walked to her, then stopped a few feet away. "Are you okay?"

"Yes. Fine. *Perfectly* fine." She seemed to be over-pronouncing her words.

"You don't look fine. You're kind of flushed. And you're acting really weird."

She put her hands to her cheeks. "Am I?"

The shower room door opened and Deacon strode out. Tobias looked at him, then back at Cassidy.

"What's going on here?"

Cassidy shook her head. "I heard singing. I thought it was you. But it was Deacon."

Tobias thought for a moment. "Deacon only sings when he's in the shower."

She glanced toward Deacon, who was fully dressed, then blushed and looked away.

Tobias smiled at her. "Was he in the shower?"

"Not anymore."

Deacon put a hand on Tobias' shoulder. "Don't worry. She turned around so fast she damn near screwed herself into the ground."

He kept walking and Cassidy ventured a look at his back, then glanced at Tobias.

He grinned. "Okay. Do you need a minute?"

"No. I'm fine." She glanced at Deacon again, and Tobias took her arm. "Let's go. You need to walk this off."

She walked with Tobias toward the exit. And when she passed Deacon, he tipped his hat at her. She scowled and kept walking.

Deacon laughed and went to Santiago's stall. The horse came to greet him. Deacon rubbed his nose. "You're lucky you've been gelded. You may not think so. But it's true. No women. No family to worry about. No female to drive you crazy." The stallion a few stalls down stomped his feet and whinnied loudly. "You should go have a beer with Bright sometime. He'll tell you all about it."

Abby came up behind him. "Talking to the horses again?"

"Yeah. They're good listeners and they don't talk back." He glanced at her. "Where are you off to?"

"Skyler and I are going for a ride."

"Skyler, huh?"

"Yes. And you don't need to worry about him. We're just friends. And even so, he's afraid to touch me. You and Tobias have him so scared."

Deacon grinned. "Good. You don't want to get involved with a Harvard man, anyway."

"You and your stupid rivalry. I'm going to have to start a list. No ivy league guys and no cowboys."

"That leaves quite a few normal guys that fit in between those two things."

Skyler came into the barn, leading his horse, Belvedere. "These Yale guys can't help themselves. They're so jealous of us, it's their only defense."

Abby shook her head. "Oh, my God. Stop. Both of you."

Deacon laughed. "Where are you going?"

"We're going to go see your new bull in action?"

"What?"

Abby laughed. "Just trying to get your attention. We're going to Angel Falls before it snows."

"Okay. I'll know where to send the search party if you don't come back."

"Between the two of us, we've got more years in the saddle than you do. Besides, you taught me how to ride. So if I'm not good, that's on you."

Deacon kissed her on the forehead. "Have a nice ride."

"We will. We'll be back for dinner."

He looked at Skyler. "You're joining us for dinner?"

"Yeah."

Abby smiled at him. "So is Cassidy. Seems everyone is going to have a friend but you."

"That's because I don't have any friends." He thought about it. "That's probably not a good thing, right?"

"Cassidy tried to be your friend. But you turned back into grumpy, distracted Deacon as soon as the gala weekend was over."

"Cassidy has Tobias. She doesn't need me to be her friend."

"Are you sure about that?"

"Of course I'm sure. Why?"

"I don't think Cassidy knows what she wants."

"What makes you say that?"

Abby shrugged. "Just a hunch. See you at dinner."

They left leading their horses, and Deacon turned back to Santiago again. "See what I mean? Women are crazy. Steer clear of them."

When he heard someone behind him, Deacon turned to see his mother. Faith never came to the barn. He couldn't remember the last time she'd left the yard. She liked her flower beds. And she liked to sit on the porch. But she steered clear of the barn. The barn had horses in it. Faith didn't like horses.

Deacon went to her. "Mother. What are you doing out here?" He took her arm and turned her toward the door.

"I'm looking for your father. I don't want him to be late for dinner. We're having guests tonight."

Deacon started her moving. Once or twice a year, she'd forget the last ten years. During those times, in her mind, her husband was alive and well. It seemed like it was happening more often this last year.

"Come on. Let me get you back to the house. I'll make sure Dad makes it to dinner on time."

"Thank you, honey." She patted his arm, and Deacon could tell that in her eyes he was twenty years old.

He walked her to the house and helped her up the steps. When he opened the front door, Ruthie was headed out. She looked relieved to see them, and she took Faith's arm.

"Where have you been, Mrs. Carmichael? You had me worried." She glanced at Deacon and he shook his head.

"Can you take her to her room? She's going to need her medication."

Faith looked at him. "I don't want to miss dinner."

"Just take a little rest, Mother."

"Okay. Send Clint in when he comes home."

"Yes, ma'am. I will."

He watched Ruthie take Faith into her room. It killed him to see her like that. But it was the only time she was happy. Her husband was alive.

He crossed the living room and went into the kitchen. It smelled heavenly, and he lifted the lid off a pot on the stove.

"Keep your fingers out of that, young man."

He put the lid down and looked at Ruthie. "I had no intention of sticking my fingers in it. Did she settle down?"

"Yes. I gave her two pills she'll most likely sleep the rest of the day."

"It seems my mother is getting worse, Ruthie."

She put a hand on his arm. "She goes through phases. She'll snap back."

Deacon wasn't so sure about that. Her phases were lasting longer and longer. With shorter periods of snapping back time.

He nodded toward the pot on the stove. "What is it?"

"It's a new recipe. Irish stew."

"With lamb?"

"Yes."

"Don't tell Abby or Tanner it's lamb. They won't eat it."

"I know those two, don't you worry. They'll never know it isn't Carmichael beef." He lifted a towel draped over something on the counter and she slapped his hand. "The bread's rising. Don't mess with it."

Deacon laughed. "Fine. Why are you so on edge, Ruthie?"

She went to the stove and stirred her stew. "It's not often we get guests for dinner anymore."

"Right. Skyler and Cassidy."

She turned and looked at him. "You behave yourself tonight."

"I always behave myself. Tobias is the troublemaker, remember?"

"I know what Tobias is capable of. But when you get in one of your moods..."

"I'll be nice. I promise." He took a glass from the cupboard and dropped two ice cubes in it. "I'll be in my office until dinner."

"Okay." She eyed the glass. "Don't you overindulge now."

"Once again, wrong brother."

He went to his office and poured a double shot of scotch over the ice, then sat at his desk. He took a sip, then smiled as he thought about the look on Cassidy's face when she walked in on him.

He liked her. He liked her a lot. And there wasn't a damn thing he could do about it.

Chapter Eighteen

"All's fair in love and war."

Despite Ruthie's request, Deacon was on his second double shot when he heard everyone arrive for dinner. He just knew he wouldn't be able to sit at the table with Cassidy and Tobias, along with everyone else, and pretend everything was okay. Everything wasn't okay.

He finished the scotch in his glass and set it on his desk. When his door opened, he looked up to see Tobias coming in.

Tobias smiled. "Hey, brother. Dinner's ready." He nodded at the empty glass. "I thought I was the drinker in the family."

Deacon looked at him. "Just my usual scotch before dinner."

Tobias walked to the desk. "You generally have a shot. By the looks of the melted ice in that glass, you've had a bit more than a shot."

"You can tell by my ice?"

He smiled. "No. But I can tell by looking at you. You're not a very good drunk."

"I'm far from being drunk."

"Maybe. Let's go eat. I think I'm the only one who'll notice your slight intoxication."

Deacon got to his feet. "After you." He followed Tobias and halfway through the living room, he whispered, "I'm not drunk."

"I believe you."

They went into the formal dining room and Deacon sat at the head of the table, with Tobias and Cassidy on one side and Abby, Skyler, and Tanner on the other.

Tanner looked at the empty seat at the other end of the table. "Where's Mother?"

Deacon put his napkin on his lap. "Mother isn't feeling well. She sends her apologies to everyone."

Everyone nodded, but he knew they were all aware of what was really going on. There was only one reason Mother would be missing dinner with invited guests. There was a large bowl of salad in the middle of the table. And next to it was a soup tureen with tomato soup. Abby stood and served salad to anyone who wanted it, then sat back down. Tobias, who didn't have salad, filled a bowl with soup, then crumbled crackers into it. He then added pepper and a dash of Tabasco sauce.

Deacon ate his salad and tried to think of something to say to fill the silence in the room. Tobias, however, came up with a subject first.

"Man, that bull is really taking care of business."

Deacon scowled at him. "Really Tobias?

He shrugged. "Just breaking the ice. He's actually just standing around waiting for November to roll around."

"Throw a smaller stone next time." Deacon looked at Abby. "Did you make it all the way to the falls?"

"Yes. It was beautiful."

Skyler nodded. "I've never been up there. It was a nice ride. Is the water ever warm enough to swim in?"

Tobias laughed. "Middle of summer, it's great. Deacon and I used to go there after chasing cows all day and take a swim."

Deacon took a drink of water. "It's been a few years since we did that."

"Yeah. That was before you forgot how to have fun." Tobias glanced at Cassidy. "We should take a ride up there before it gets too cold."

"It's much too cold to swim. And I'm not too fond of water I can't see the bottom of."

He grinned. "The water at the bottom of the falls is crystal clear. You can see down..." He looked at Deacon. "What? Ten feet?"

"About that."

"In that case, it'd be nice. But no swimming until next summer. When does the weather change?"

Deacon pushed his half-eaten salad away. "Any day now." He didn't like that she'd alluded to a future with Tobias.

The conversation turned to other good places to ride, then Skyler told them about playing Polo at Harvard. He obviously enjoyed the sport and missed it. He went on for quite a while about the intricacies of the sport. Then he and Tobias spent a fair amount of time comparing the sport to rodeo and equestrian events.

Deacon half-listened to everyone. He just wanted dinner to be over with. He didn't add anything, and only responded if he was addressed directly. When he spotted Ruthie in the doorway waving at him, he jumped at the opportunity to escape.

"Excuse me. I'm being summoned."

When he got into the kitchen, she put her hands on her hips. "I told you to be nice."

"What did I do?"

"Nothing. You've been sitting there like a toad on a log."

Even though Deacon was twenty-three when his father died and his mother checked out, he still needed a motherly figure in his life. Ruthie had filled that void. She'd been with the Carmichaels since before Deacon was born, so it was a natural transition from cook to nanny. Or in Deacon's case, someone to go to when he needed advice.

He folded his arms across his chest. "How do you know I'm not doing anything?"

"Do you think I just sit in the kitchen during these dinners? I was eavesdropping, of course."

He smiled. He loved Ruthie as much as he did any other member of the family. "I'm sorry I wasn't more entertaining for you."

"You're the head of the family. Go be sociable."

Deacon sighed. "Not really feeling that sociable, Ruthie."

She cocked her head at him, then leaned in close. "It's Miss Cassidy, isn't it?"

He tried not to react to her intuition, which was usually spot on. "What about her?"

"All's fair in love and war."

"No. It's not."

"Because Mr. Tobias is sweet on her too?"

"You make it sound like we're in high school."

"Well, you two boys are acting like you are. Don't you think Miss Cassidy has a right to choose which one of you lovesick cowboys she wants to spend her time with?"

"Ruthie. I appreciate your input. But it's a lot more complicated than that." He picked up a lemon square from the tray on the counter and headed for the back door.

Ruthie frowned at him. "Hey. Who's going to help me with the dessert?"

"Ask Tobias. He's currently the man of the hour."

———— ❦ ————

After dinner, Cassidy and Tobias took a walk down the driveway. It was a half-mile of gravel road with rows of oak trees along either side. It was dark, but the moon was almost full and provided enough light to see by.

Tobias took her hand. "Sorry about Deacon. He doesn't usually disappear in the middle of dinner with guests."

"It's fine. He seems to be distracted these days. He must have a lot on his mind."

"I guess." They stopped, and Tobias took her other hand. "Seems like a pretty good place to catch a kiss or two." He leaned in and she put a hand on his chest to stop him. He took a step back. "What's wrong?"

"I'm sorry." She took a step back from him, as well. "I'm really, really sorry." She swallowed the lump in her throat. She didn't want to get emotional. But this was going to be really hard.

"For what?"

She took a breath to calm her nerves. "I know you like me. And I have loved spending time with you."

He let go of her hands. "Wait. Hold on. This sounds a lot like an 'it's not you, it's me' speech. Just cut the bull and tell me straight."

She looked at him. "Okay. I don't feel the same way you do."

He looked hurt, and it broke her heart. "I thought we've been having a good time together."

"We have. You're great." The last thing she wanted to do was hurt him. But she had.

"Just not great enough? You don't think you could learn to love me? Because that's where I feel this is going. Not the love I professed the night of the gala. Real, honest to goodness love."

She turned away from him and walked to the middle of the drive. She needed a minute to collect herself. After a moment, she returned to him. "What I want is to be with someone I don't need to take time to fall in love with. I want an instant connection. I want...fireworks."

"And I don't do that for you?"

She shook her head. "No. I'm sorry." She blinked away some tears, but one escaped and ran down her cheek.

He wiped it away and took her hand again. "Quit apologizing. I'm not mad. Or upset." He thought for a moment. "Well, that's a lie. I'm upset. But I get it. I think. I don't want you to cry, though. That I can't take."

She put her arms around him and hugged him. "There's someone out there for you. And when you find her, when you feel the fireworks go off, you'll know she's the one."

He held her tight. "So does this mean you've found your someone?"

"No. And maybe I never will. Maybe it's an impossible idea to go after. But I need to try. I need to wait and take a chance he's out there somewhere."

"Well, whoever the hell he is, he's a damn lucky son of a bitch."

She let go of him. "I really wish it was you."

"Probably not as much as I do." He stuck his hands in his pockets. "We should head back."

"You go ahead. I'm going to stay here for a few minutes. Then I'm going to go home."

"Are you sure?"

She nodded.

"Okay. You take care Cassidy."

"You too, Tobias."

She watched him until she could no longer see him in the darkness. She hated hurting him. But she couldn't continue a relationship with him being so unsure over how she felt about Deacon. She hadn't as yet felt the fireworks, but the kiss in her grandfather's barn, and the shower incident had started a flame that certainly had the possibility of setting off a whole string of fireworks. Of course figuring this all out would be a lot easier if Deacon hadn't shut down on her and closed her out.

***

Deacon was sitting on the rail of the training pen when Tobias came up behind him. He climbed up and sat next to him.

"You know there isn't a horse in there, right?"

"Just counting stars." He glanced at Tobias. "Where's Cassidy?"

"She went home."

It wasn't terrible news, but it didn't seem right. "Really? Kind of early."

"Yeah. Right after she broke up with me. Not that we were officially together."

Deacon turned toward him. "What? What are you talking about?"

"It's fine. I kind of understand her reasoning."

"Which is?"

"That I didn't bring on the fireworks."

"What do you mean?"

"I'm not the one. Plain and simple."

"I'm really sorry." He was. This isn't what he wanted. Tobias deserved to have someone like Cassidy in his life. She'd be really good for him.

Tobias shrugged. *"C'est la vie."*

Deacon put a hand on his shoulder. "I'm glad to see all the money I spent on your education paid off." He took a moment. "Seriously. I'm sorry, man. But I wouldn't give up. She's just confused. She'll change her mind."

"I don't think so. Seems her mind is pretty made up. I really thought she might be my one." He laughed. "That's what I get for thinking I could be anyone's one."

"There's someone out there for everyone, Tobias."

"Do you really believe that?"

"Yes. I do."

"So why aren't you out there looking for yours?"

"Just because I know she's out there somewhere doesn't mean I want to go looking for her. Or even deserve her."

Tobias looked up at the stars. "Are we going to die as two shriveled up bachelor cowboys?"

Deacon laughed. "I don't know about you, but I plan on going out as the silver haired devil all the ladies in the old folks' home can't keep their hands off of."

"Sounds like a plan. Count me in. Can we get matching canes?"

"No."

Chapter Nineteen

"No. Yes. Sort of."

Tobias pretended he was fine, but Deacon knew he wasn't. How could he be? An incredible woman just told him he wasn't the one she wanted. So, Tobias spent the days working hard, and spent the nights drinking a little too much rum. But Deacon left him to it. Who was he to judge? Tobias had to work through it himself. Unless there was something Deacon could do about it.

His mind kicked into fix-it mode. He could fix this. Cassidy was just confused because of the kiss they shared. She had it in her head he was going to change his mind. That he was the one she wanted. He did want her. But it was too late for that. Tobias set his sights on her first. There was no way he could pursue Cassidy without it looking like he was stabbing Tobias in the back. Family came first.

He had to go see her and set things right. The problem was, he didn't quite trust himself around her. The dreams had returned, and she was always on his mind. No matter how hard he tried to distract himself, his mind always wandered back to her. He needed a safe space to talk some sense into her. The most innocuous place to have that conversation with her would be the classroom. He'd go after school and catch her before she left for the day.

It took him four days to get up the courage. But when Thursday arrived, he knew he had to do it. He and Tobias were headed to Abilene Friday morning for the big annual Abilene Roundup. It was a horse show and auction, with a dinner Saturday night followed by cocktails and a mixer. They went every year and he had to go. So Thursday morning, he told Tanner he'd pick him up from school, but he needed to talk with Cassidy first.

Tanner was confused. "Am I in trouble?"

"No. It has nothing to do with you. Just meet me by my truck after school."

Deacon spent the day working with a particularly hard-headed horse. It kept his mind occupied. But as the end of the school day drew near, he returned the horse to the barn and headed to the house for a shower. He got to the school as the bell was ringing, and he passed the exiting students, going against traffic, until he got into the hallway. He walked to Cassidy's room, hesitating at the door, before opening it.

She was at her desk and she seemed surprised to see him.

"Deacon? What brings you here?"

"Can I come in?"

"Of course."

He stepped inside and closed the door behind him. "I, ah... I wanted to talk to you about something."

She stood and came around the desk. "Is everything okay?"

He nodded. "Yeah. Well, no, actually."

"Is it Tobias?"

"No. Yes. Sort of." He looked at her. She looked really nice in a yellow blouse the same color as her dress from the gala. "Shit."

She moved closer to him. "Deacon. What is it?"

He took a deep breath and blew it out slowly. "I think you should reconsider breaking up with Tobias."

She looked surprised. "That's between him and me. Why do you care?"

"I think you're whole, 'looking for fireworks' is a little misguided."

"He told you what I said?"

"Not all of it. Just the fireworks thing."

"You don't think love should be powerful and all-consuming?"

Of course he did. He was feeling it right now. And he wished they were in a much bigger room, so he could put more distance between them. "No. I don't. I think love is constant and quiet. It's wanting to take care of someone. It's having someone you can talk to about everything and nothing. It's wanting to stay awake at night just to keep talking to them. And wake up early to watch them as they rouse from their sleep. It's... Dammit."

He closed the space between them in two steps and pulled her into him. Then he kissed her like he'd never kissed anyone before. After a few moments, he let go of her and took a step back.

"Okay. I was wrong about the fireworks."

She smiled and moved toward him. He backed up a step. "No. Please, stay there."

"Deacon. I don't want to be with Tobias. I want to be with you. I want to be the one you fall asleep with and wake up to. I want to talk with you about everything and nothing. I want a quiet and constant love that is also powerful and all consuming. You felt the fireworks. How can that be wrong?"

"Don't say that."

"Why? You deserve to be happy as much as anyone else. You think we can't be together because Tobias and I spent some time together? Don't I get a say in this? This is my heart we're talking about, too. I understand your loyalty to Tobias. But in this instance, I think he'd understand. Don't you think he'd want you to be happy? That I deserve to be happy?"

He looked at the ground for a moment, then at Cassidy. "I can't stop thinking about you."

She moved toward him again, and this time he didn't move away. They embraced again, and he whispered in her ear. "I can only be so strong."

"What the hell?" Deacon and Cassidy stepped away from each other to find Tobias standing in the doorway. "Okay. Now I get it."

Deacon raised a hand. "It's not what it looks like."

"Really? Because it looks like you two were about to get down and dirty right here in the classroom."

Deacon glanced at Cassidy, then back at Tobias. "Watch your mouth, Tobias."

Tobias looked at Cassidy. "Sorry. I guess I see what you meant about fireworks. There were sparks flying all over this room."

Cassidy moved toward him. "Tobias, let's sit down and talk about this."

"No. I need to leave before I say...or do, something I'll regret." He turned then and left the room, closing the door hard, behind him.

Cassidy turned to Deacon. "Deacon?"

"I need to go. I'll talk to him. Once he cools down, that is."

"What about us? What about what just happened?"

"I don't know, Cassidy. I honestly don't know."

"We need to talk."

"And we will. Next week."

"Next week?"

"Yeah. Tobias and I are headed to Abilene for an auction tomorrow morning. We'll be gone until Monday."

"Monday?"

"I'll call you."

"Okay."

"I need to go and make sure he doesn't do anything stupid."

"Please call me later."

He nodded, then left the room. Cassidy leaned on her desk, then put her face in her hands.

She was still crying when the door opened again.

When she looked up and saw Tanner, she turned away from him and wiped her eyes.

"Miss O'Hare. Are you okay?"

She nodded.

"Are you sure?" He came into the room. He was down to one crutch and his cast had been replaced by a soft boot.

She turned back to him and tried to give him a reassuring smile. "Yes. Sorry."

"Don't be. Can I help?"

"No. I'm fine, really. What do you need?"

"Well, when I left class, I saw both Deacon and Tobias' trucks. But I went to the office for a minute and when I came to the parking lot, they were both gone."

"One of them was supposed to bring you home?"

"Yeah. Deacon. But he left me."

Cassidy went behind her desk and gathered her things. "I'll take you. Something must have come up." She took a tissue and wiped her eyes and blew her nose, then tossed it in the waste can.

"Are you sure?"

"Yes." She crossed the room and opened the door. She held it for him. "I'm sure."

Tanner was quiet until they were halfway to the ranch. He glanced at Cassidy.

"I know everyone assumes I don't know what's going on. But I'm not stupid."

"Of course you're not."

"I know you're not with Tobias anymore."

She looked at him when they stopped at a stop sign. "That's right, I'm not."

He was quiet for a moment. "You like Deacon, don't you?"

She considered lying to him, denying the truth, but she couldn't. She didn't want to deny it anymore. "Yes, I do."

Tanner nodded. "He likes you too. And I think he has since the gala."

She felt the tears coming, and she swallowed hard to stop them. "I'm not sure how it's all going to turn out."

"You have to understand Deacon. He feels responsible for all of us. When Dad died, and Mother...well, she hasn't been the same since. He thinks he has to be strong for all of us. He thinks he has to sacrifice his happiness in order to make sure we're all happy."

"Tanner, you're wise beyond your years."

"I just keep my eyes open. Everyone thinks because I'm a kid, they don't need to include me in everything. Like they're somehow protecting me." He looked at her. "I don't need to be protected."

"I'm sure you don't. It's because they love you, though."

He took a deep breath. "Deacon deserves to be happy. And if you make him happy, then it's up to you to make him see it."

"I don't know how to do that."

He thought for a moment. "Just don't take no for an answer."

Cassidy smiled. "If only it was that easy."

"It is easy. Adults complicate everything. They take something simple, like love, and muddle it up with crap that doesn't mean anything in the long run."

Cassidy reached for his arm. "Thank you, Tanner, for giving me some clarity."

"Did I really? Or are you just saying that?"

"I don't know how your family survived what it has and still produced four exceptional human beings."

"I'm not exceptional."

"Of course you are. You're a Carmichael. Just like your brothers. Just like Abby. Your father would be so proud to see how you've all turned out."

"So, what are you going to do about Deacon?"

"I guess I'm not going to take no for an answer."

Tanner grinned. "Maybe someday you'll be a Carmichael, too."

"That would be an honor."

Chapter Twenty

"He who has the most money wins."

Abby found Deacon in the barn filling large plastic containers from sacks of grain. The plastic kept the mice out and made it easier to give it to the horses. It wasn't a job Deacon normally did. She watched him for a moment before saying anything.

"So here you are again, doing a job that we pay the hands to do."

He set the scoop aside, then emptied the rest of the bag into the container. "Just keeping busy."

"Right. Because you have so much downtime. Filling the grain barrel falls into the same category as mucking out stalls. What's going on? And don't say nothing. Tanner and I were the only two children at dinner. Mother was quite confused."

"Is she okay?"

"Yes. I told her you guys were getting ready for the roundup."

"Good."

"Which was a lie. Ruthie said you grabbed a sandwich and went out the back door. And I saw Tobias head upstairs with a bottle of rum. What's up?"

He tossed the empty sack into a garbage can, then sat on a bale of hay. "How'd you like to go to the roundup with us?"

She couldn't believe he was actually asking her. She'd been begging him to let her go for the last three years. "Seriously? Oh, my gosh. Of course." She cocked her head. "Wait a minute. Why? Why this year? You're avoiding telling me what's going on with you and Tobias."

"Tobias and I might need a buffer. He's currently really pissed at me. And deservedly so."

"What did you do?"

"Nothing you need to worry about."

She put her hands on her hips. "If I'm being your buffer. I need to know why."

He picked at the hay for a moment. "I kissed Cassidy."

She sat down on another hay bale. "You did what, now? Have you been seeing her behind his back?"

"No. Of course not. You know me better than that. He knows me better than that, too. And once he gets his head straight, he'll realize it. But for now, it's going to be a pretty icy weekend."

"I need all the details."

Deacon frowned. "I'll give you the abridged version."

"Fine. But don't leave out the kiss. I need to hear about the kiss."

"Cassidy and I have been slightly drawn to each other since the gala."

"Slightly drawn to each other?"

"If you're going to repeat everything I say this is going to take all night."

"Fine. Go ahead."

"But I know it can't happen. I made it quite clear." Abby opened her mouth to say something, but closed it. Deacon sighed. "But the day after Queenie foaled, there was a kiss. Not a life-changing kiss. Just a kiss. It was a mistake."

"Okay. That seems harmless enough, I guess. So how'd Tobias find out about it?"

"He didn't. He doesn't know about that one."

"Deacon!"

"Let me finish before you judge me." He took another breath. "When she broke up with Tobias, I figured I needed to go talk to her. I didn't want her breaking up with him because of me. Or for me."

She scowled at him. "You're kind of conceited."

"Do you want to hear the rest of the story or not?" She nodded, and he went on. "So today, I went to the school to talk to her in the classroom. A safe space. Nothing could be construed or taken out of context. Only..." He got to his feet and leaned against a stall. "Only. One thing led to another, and there was a kiss. Two actually. And Tobias walked in on the second one."

Abby pulled her knees up onto the hay and hugged them. "I'm assuming this was more than just a kiss."

"A hell of a lot more, yeah."

Abby smiled. "Oh, my God. You're in love with her."

"How the hell did you come to that conclusion?"

"It's so obvious. I don't know why I didn't see it sooner. The mighty Deacon has fallen."

"You're not helping. I need to fix this."

Abby stood and went to him. "There's no fixing this. When Tobias figures out that this is love. That you two love each other, he'll come around. He won't hate you forever. And he won't stand in your way."

"I can't be with Cassidy."

"Why?" When he didn't answer, she took his hand. "You've been taking care of this family for ten years. You've put everything you have into it. And in the process, you've missed out on having a life of your own. You're due, Deacon. This is your shot."

Tobias walked into the barn, saw them, then turned and walked out. Deacon started after him, but Abby took his arm.

"Let him be. He needs time to figure this out on his own."

"He thinks I stole his girl."

Abby shook her head. "Right now, he might think that. But like you said, once he gets his head straight, he'll know better."

"I guess."

"So, what time are we leaving in the morning?"

"Nine."

She squealed. "Yay. I'm going to go pack." She headed for the door, then turned and went back to Deacon. She put her arms around his neck and hugged him. "Thank you for telling me."

"I figured I harass you whenever you do something stupid. It's about time I admit to doing my own stupid shit."

"Deacon. I know you do stupid shit. But this isn't that. This is a good thing."

"I don't see how."

"Go call her. I'm sure you went running out of there without talking about what happened."

"Yeah. I did."

"Call her."

Deacon left the barn and went to his office to pour himself a double shot of scotch. Then he headed upstairs to his room. He sat on the couch and stared at the unlit fireplace. He took a sip of scotch, then picked up his phone.

Cassidy answered on the second ring. "Deacon?"

"Hi."

"Is everything okay over there? Have you talked to Tobias?"

"No. He doesn't want to talk to me. Can we talk about anything else besides what happened this afternoon? Tell me about your day up to that point. Tell me about Queenie and Precious. Anything. Just talk to me."

She did as he asked, and they talked for the next two hours about everything and nothing. When they both started yawning, Cassidy suggested they call it a night.

"Not yet. Let me tell you about my weekend."

He spent another thirty minutes telling her about what he, Tobias, and Abby would be doing over the next three days.

"I guess that's it. We're leaving in the morning and we'll be back late Sunday night."

"Drive safe."

"Always. Thank you."

"For what?"

"Talking to me."

"I'll always talk to you, Deacon."

"Good night, Cassidy."

"Good night."

Tobias still wasn't talking to Deacon the next morning, and he was quite hungover. So he slept most of the way while Deacon drove. Tobias took the backseat, so Abby sat next to Deacon and chatted the whole way. Usually, Abby's chatting got to Deacon. But today, it was a welcome distraction. They pulled into Abilene at one o'clock and parked in the hotel lot where some of the activities would be taking place. Deacon had reserved three consecutive rooms on the same floor. Tobias took his key and opened his door.

He looked at Abby. "I'll see you at dinner." He went into his room and closed the door.

Abby glanced at Deacon. "Off to a great start." They stopped at the middle room next. "Do I really have to sit in my room all afternoon?"

"There's a pool."

"I know. I brought a suit."

"Go have fun. Just stay on the hotel grounds, don't let any of these rich bastard cowboys sweet talk you, and don't be late for dinner. If you're not there, I'm pretty sure Tobias won't eat with me."

"Understood."

"I'll see you at six."

"What are you going to do?"

"Go to the bar. Mingle."

"Your favorite thing to do."

———————————⬡———————————

Abby changed into her swimsuit, before heading for the pool. She found a chaise that wasn't too close to anyone else and got comfortable. Then she took the book she brought out of her bag and started reading. She'd made it through a few chapters when she heard a familiar voice.

"What the hell is Abby Carmichael doing at the roundup?"

She lowered her book and smiled at Skyler. "I could ask you the same question. Last I talked to you, you weren't coming."

He dragged a chaise over and sat on the end of it. He was wearing swim trunks and a t-shirt. He looked good with his blond hair in the sun, and his sunglasses. He could've been on a beach in California and fit right in. Abby suddenly felt self-conscious in her swimsuit. It was a tankini and fairly conservative bottoms, but still, she felt vulnerable.

He smiled at her. "Looking good, Miss Carmichael."

"You're not so bad yourself, Mr. Fremont. Did your plans fall through? How are you here?"

"My dad insisted I come. So, I canceled my plans and here I am. Because like a good son, I do what my bastard father tells me to do."

"I don't know why you don't like it. I can't wait until tomorrow."

He shrugged. "It's just the same old elitism we saw at the gala. A lot of the same people. Same games. He who has the most money wins."

"That'd be your family. So congratulations."

"Well, according to my dad, the Carmichaels are inching closer every day."

"Good to know. Do you need to eat with your father tonight, or can you come eat with my brothers and me?"

"Actually, I can. Dad's having a private dinner." He leaned toward Abby. "I'm pretty sure he's having an affair."

"No way."

"Afraid so." He shrugged. "Don't really care much one way or the other. I think my mom's been sleeping with the tennis pro at the club."

"Skyler. That's horrible."

"That's the Fremonts. You don't know how lucky you are to have a semi-normal family."

Abby thought about her mother. No one outside of the family knew how bad she'd gotten over the years. "You're right. I'll give you a little Carmichael gossip, though, if you want."

"Absolutely. Tell me."

"Deacon and Tobias aren't talking to each other. He only asked me to come to be a buffer between them."

"What happened?"

"Cassidy O'Hare happened."

"How so?"

"Seems both my brothers are smitten by her."

"Interesting."

"You can't say anything."

"I'd never. As you probably already know, I'm a little scared of your brothers."

Abby smiled. "So, you up for dinner with the feuding Carmichael brothers?"

"I'll be there."

Deacon had the obligatory drink in his hand while he shook hands with fellow ranchers, horse dealers, and horse trainers. Some had their spouses, some were with women their wives didn't know about, and some were single like Deacon. He hated these things, and he had to go to another more formal one after dinner, that'd have even more of the same types of people.

When Scott Bonner approached with a smile, Deacon shook with him. Scott raised horses, and had a good reputation for quality stock.

"How're you doing, Scott?"

"Good. I've got a stallion I'd like to give you first shot at."

"Not really in the market for one, but I'll take a look."

"Come find me tomorrow morning before the auction. "I think you'll be impressed. His sire is Caspian."

"Nice. Is he solid black, then?"

"No. He has one white sock. If he was pure black, I'd probably get more for him."

"I'll track you down tomorrow and take a look at him."

Scott wandered off and Deacon checked his watch. He'd done his due diligence. Dinner was in an hour. He had time to go to his room and relax for a bit, before sitting at the dinner table with Tobias.

Deacon got to the dinner a few minutes late and found Tobias sitting next to Abby. He took the seat on the other side of her and she gave him a smile.

"Seems I remember you telling me not to be late."

"I fell asleep."

"I thought you went to the bar to schmooze."

"I did. Then I came back to my room and sat on the tiny little patio overlooking the pool. And I dozed off."

"Too much scotch?"

"Maybe a little."

Abby glanced at Tobias. "And what did you do this afternoon?"

"I went to look at the horses. There are a few good ones might be worth bidding on."

Deacon looked around Abby. "Did you see Scott Bonner's stallion? He was trying to get me interested in him."

Tobias shook his head.

Deacon sighed. "Okay."

Abby looked at Deacon and raised an eyebrow. "So, guess who I ran into at the pool?" When neither of her brothers ventured a guess, she continued talking. "Skyler. His dad made him come."

Tobias grumbled. "His bastard father waits to see what we bid on, then raises the price until the horse isn't worth bidding on anymore."

Deacon smiled. "We should bid on Scott's stallion."

Abby looked at him. "Because you don't really want it?"

"Yep."

The waiter came by and put their meals down in front of them. Tobias dug in and was quiet for the rest of the evening. Skyler never showed, which Abby found disappointing. But she wasn't sure why.

When they were done eating, they returned to their rooms. Tobias went into his after saying goodnight to Abby.

When they got to her door, she looked at Deacon. "Kind of early."

"Big day tomorrow. Get some sleep."

"A big day with Mr. Happy?"

"Yeah."

"Maybe you should try to talk to him."

"Trust me. He's not ready to talk."

Chapter Twenty-One

"Ouch. That stung a little."

On Saturday, Tobias was a no show at the clinics and the horsemanship games. Deacon hoped he wasn't drinking himself into oblivion. The big event of the weekend, aside from the auction was the benefit dinner. He hoped Tobias would show and not be drunk.

Abby and Deacon attended the hundred dollar a plate dinner, which was a formal affair. Since Abby had no notice she was attending the roundup, she brought the dress she wore to the gala. Deacon wore a suit. The event to benefit a horse riding program for special needs children was well attended. Along with dinner, there was a silent auction, a cash bar, and live music.

Tobias showed up a few minutes late and Abby sat between them again. She was excited by the glamor of it all.

Deacon smiled at her. "What do you think?"

"This is awesome."

"How is this different from the gala? A bunch of rich bastards, hanging out talking about horses, fine wine, and old bourbon."

"Well, at least it's for a good cause."

"That's true."

"Can we bid on something in the silent auction?"

"Eat your hundred dollar steak first."

She leaned in close. "It's not very good."

He grinned. "That's because it's not Carmichael beef."

"That must be it."

When he noticed her looking around for someone specific, he smiled. "Looking for Skyler?"

"He said he'd be here."

"I'm sure he'll show. Leo Fremont won't miss this opportunity to show everyone how generous he can be." Deacon nudged her. "Talk to your other brother. Everyone is starting to notice his sulking in silence routine."

After dinner, they went to check out the items offered for the silent auction. Most of it was either boring, too good to have a chance of winning, or something they weren't interested in. But when Abby spotted a beautifully tooled Mexican saddle that was died a dark burgundy, she went to it.

"That. That's what I want."

Tobias looked at it. "Why?"

"Because it's beautiful and I've always wanted one."

"I doubt anyone else is going to bid on it, so go for it."

She looked at Deacon. "Can we place a bid?"

He glanced at Tobias. "Yeah, sure, if that's what you want." He picked up a slip of paper and filled it out with Abby's name and the bid of one thousand dollars.

She hugged his arm. "Thank you."

Tobias shook his head. "Probably could've gotten it for a couple hundred bucks."

Deacon folded the paper and put it into the bid box. "This is Abby's first roundup. She should go home with something."

Tobias shrugged. "It's your money. Oh wait, no it's not. It's our money."

Deacon took his arm. "You can be pissed at me all you want. And for as long as you want. But you're not going to disrespect this function or our family by being an asshole."

Tobias pulled his arm away and walked down the table, then stopped in front of the big prize for the night. An Arabian gelding. He picked up a bid slip. "Well, let's support the cause and send Abby home with a fancy horse to put her fancy saddle on."

Deacon moved down the table to him. "We don't need an Arabian horse. We'll be buying horses tomorrow at the auction for a good price."

Tobias looked at him for a moment, then filled out the form and dropped it in the box.

"That's for you, Abby." He walked away then and Abby turned to Deacon.

"Can you get that back? God knows what he bid."

Deacon shook his head. "No. Let's just hope there's someone else crazier than him here tonight."

There wasn't. The Carmichaels left the benefit dinner with a Mexican saddle and an Arabian horse. Judging by the thank you handshake Deacon got when he went to collect the paperwork on the horse, Tobias' temper tantrum had cost a lot. He'd find out how much on Monday when the funds came out of the bank.

Tobias retired shortly after and Abby decided to call it a night, too. But Deacon needed to do a little more schmoozing before he could retire. He headed for the bar and spent two hours drinking with people he barely knew, and most of whom he didn't like. When the place started to clear out, he sat at the bar to have one more. He'd already had too many, so he figured one more couldn't hurt.

When someone sat down next to him, he glanced over, then turned in his seat. It was Rachel Steel, the woman he almost married.

"Hey there, handsome."

"Rachel? What the hell are you doing here?"

"I have a ranch, too."

"Right. You inherited it when your husband died."

"Buy me a drink, Deacon."

Deacon waved at the bartender. "Two more."

"You remember what I drink."

"You introduced me to scotch. Of course I remember."

Rachel had blown into his life when he was twenty-two. He was fresh out of college and he couldn't believe a woman like her would be interested in him. Six months later, he figured out she wasn't. She was after the Carmichael's money. She'd since married a man much older than herself, and he conveniently died five years later, leaving his ranch to her.

She put a hand on his arm. "I haven't seen you since the funeral."

"My father's or your husband's?"

"Both I guess."

The bartender put two scotches down on the bar, and Deacon signed the tab. He raised his glass and Rachel tapped it.

She smiled. "To old times." She took a drink. "So I hear you're still single. How is that possible?"

Cassidy popped into his mind. "And planning to stay that way."

"Such a shame. But that does leave you free to revisit past *histoire d'amour*."

"Not really interested in dredging up my past mistakes."

"Ouch. That stung a little."

After two more drinks, Deacon was reconsidering his *histoire d'amour* with Rachel. Maybe it's what he needed to get Cassidy off his mind. If he did something to make himself unworthy of her, it'd be easier to walk away. He ordered two more drinks.

He couldn't remember how it happened, but when he had a lucid moment, he found himself in a cab with Rachel beside him.

"Where are we going again?"

"My hotel room. I like to stay away from the roundup crowd."

"Sure. Makes sense." He tried to clear the fog from his brain. "And why are we going to your hotel?"

She squeezed his thigh. "You're so cute."

The cab dropped them and drove off, as Rachel took Deacon's arm and led him into the lobby. They crossed the empty space to the elevator, and she pushed the up button.

Deacon was still trying to remember agreeing to this, when the doors opened and she pulled him into the elevator. She turned to him and kissed him.

"I've been waiting to do that all night."

He took a step back from her. "Wait a minute. Why are we here again?"

She whispered in his ear, and he took another step back. She never was shy when it came to describing certain acts.

He shook his head. "Yeah. That's not going to happen."

"Don't be shy now. I know what you like."

The elevator stopped, the doors opened, and Rachel smiled at him. "Come on now. My room is right down the hall. You made it this far."

Deacon shook his head. "No. I can't."

"Sure you can."

"No. I need to go."

She sighed and put a hand on the doors to keep them from closing. "Deacon Carmichael, get your ass out of the elevator."

He shook his head. "Let go of the door, Rachel."

She frowned, then stepped outside of the elevator and let the doors close. Deacon leaned against the wall for a moment, then realized he needed to push a button in order to make the damn thing move.

When he got to the lobby, he went out the front doors and made it to a bench in front of the building. He sat and closed his eyes until the world stopped spinning around him. The doorman stepped out and eyed him.

Deacon gave him a wave. "I'm good."

The man didn't look convinced, but he went back inside.

Deacon took his phone from his pocket and tried to focus on it. When he could see it, he pulled up his contacts and dialed.

Tobias answered after several rings. "Someone better be dead."

"Tobias."

"Deacon?"

"I need your help."

"Call Abby."

He ran his hand over his hair. "It's the middle of the night, man. You want me to call our little sister to come rescue me?"

"If you're in your room two doors down from mine, yes."

Deacon looked around. "I'm not at the hotel."

"Where the hell are you? It's two in the morning. Are you drunk?"

"A little, yeah." Deacon thought about it. "Actually, a lot. I'm a lot drunk."

"Where are you?"

Deacon looked around again. "I have no idea." He took a moment. "A hotel. But not our hotel." He looked at the building. "There's an S."

"An S?"

"Yeah. An S inside a shield, sort of. Kind of looks like Superman's symbol. Only fancier. Like Superman would have under a tuxedo." He laughed. "That'd be cool."

"Deacon, focus. Can you see a street name? Or better yet, a person?"

He looked around. "Not a soul." He looked toward the door. "There was a doorman, but he's gone now, and I don't think I can go find him."

"Okay, just stay put. You're safe, right?"

"Yeah. Sure. No one's around. I'm all by myself on this bench in front of Kal-El's place."

"What else is on the street? Anything you recognize?"

Deacon looked across the street. "There's a restaurant."

"What's it called?"

He squinted at the restaurant. "I don't know."

"Is there a sign?"

"Umm. Yes. There's a sign."

"And what's it say?"

Deacon tried to focus on the sign. "Ric...Ric...Ricardo's. Yeah. Ricardo's Fine Italian Dining. Sounds really good. I don't think they're open though. It's really dark inside."

"Okay. Listen to me. I'll be there soon. I'm getting up right now. Stay put."

"Brother, I couldn't go anywhere if I wanted to." He spotted the doorman again and called out to him. "Oh hey there."

"Who are you talking to?"

"The doorman's back."

"Call him over and give him the phone."

Deacon frowned. "I'm not going to give him my phone."

"Don't give it to him. Just let me talk to him for a moment."

Deacon waved at the doorman. "My brother wants to talk to you." The doorman walked over to him and Deacon handed him the phone. "My brother. He wants to talk to you."

The man took the phone. "Hello?"

Deacon couldn't hear what Tobias was saying, but whatever it was, it seemed to make the man a little less upset about the wasted man sitting in front of the hotel.

"Yes, sir. No problem." He handed the phone back to Deacon.

"Tobias?"

"Yeah. Sit tight. I'll be there in fifteen minutes."

"Gotcha." He ended the call and tucked the phone in his pocket. The doorman had moved back to his post, but stayed outside.

It seemed like only minutes before Tobias pulled up in Deacon's Jeep. He got out and went to Deacon.

"What the hell, man?"

Deacon looked up at Tobias. "You got here fast."

"Do you want to tell me how you got here?"

"Rachel."

"Rachel Steel?"

"That's the one."

"You came here with her?'

Deacon scowled. "Didn't I just say that?"

"Did you sleep with her?"

Deacon shook his head. "No. I did not sleep with her. She wanted me too. She *really* wanted me to."

"But you didn't."

"Nope."

"Why not?"

Deacon took a deep breath. "Because she's not the one."

"Which one?"

"The one I want to be with."

Tobias sat on the bench next to him. "This will probably be the best chance I have to get a straight answer from you. Do you love Cassidy?"

Deacon nodded. "Yes. I do. She's my one, Tobias."

Tobias got to his feet and took Deacon's arm. "Okay, big brother. Let's get you back to the hotel." He took Deacon to the Jeep and put him in the passenger seat. "Sit tight. I need to go talk to the doorman."

Deacon watched him hand some money to the doorman. "Easiest tip that guy ever earned."

Tobias returned to the Jeep and got in behind the wheel, then looked at Deacon. "I'm sorry, Deacon."

"For what?"

"For being an asshole about Cassidy."

"You're not the asshole. I'm the asshole."

Tobias smiled. "We'll call it a tie."

He pulled away and Deacon looked at the hotel. "Bye Kal-El."

Chapter Twenty-Two

"Shouldn't you take me to dinner first?"

Tobias got Deacon out of the car and took him through the empty lobby to the elevator. They went up to their floor, and Tobias led him down the hallway. When they got to Deacon's door, Tobias leaned him against the wall.

"Stand there. Where's your key?" Deacon patted his pockets and pulled out his car keys. "Not those keys. Your room key. It's a card."

Deacon shrugged. "I have no idea what the hell you're talking about."

Abby's door opened. "Oh, my God. What's going on?"

Deacon smiled at her. "Hey, sis."

Tobias shook his head. "Our brother is wasted." He started searching Deacon's pockets for the key.

Deacon frowned. "Shouldn't you take me to dinner first?"

Tobias pulled the key from Deacon's back pocket and looked at Abby. "Hold on to him."

Abby took Deacon's arm. "He's really plowed."

"I see that."

Deacon grinned. "Hey, Abby."

"Hi, Deacon. Where have you been?"

"With..." He lowered his voice. "Rachel."

Abby looked at Tobias, who'd just opened the door. "Rachel, Rachel?"

"Yeah. He says he didn't sleep with her."

"Ew. I hope not."

Deacon shook his head. "I didn't sleep with her. She wanted me to, though. She really wanted me to."

Abby patted his chest. "Okay. I don't need to know the details."

Tobias took Deacon's arm. "Come on. Let's get you to bed." He looked at Abby. "You can go back to your room."

"No way. I've never seen him this drunk. Or drunk at all, really. Maybe slightly toasted. But this? Wow."

Tobias took Deacon inside and set him on the bed. "Then help me get him undressed."

"Um, no."

"Not totally undressed. Take his boots off."

Abby took hold of Deacon's boot and tried working it off of his foot. "Relax your foot, Deacon."

"I'm totally relaxed, man."

She got one off, then removed the other, while Tobias took off Deacon's jacket and took his wallet and keys from his pockets. He laid Deacon down and Abby covered him with a blanket.

Deacon looked at Abby. "My brother is talking to me again."

"Good. I'm glad."

He looked at Tobias. "I didn't mean to fall in love with her. I couldn't help it."

"It's okay. I get it."

"But don't worry. I'll make it right. I'll honor the bro code."

"We'll talk about it tomorrow. Get some sleep."

Abby turned off the bedside light, then took Tobias' arm and led him to the door. "So, what did I miss?"

They went into the hall. "He ended up at Rachel's hotel across town."

"He didn't go to her room, though. Right?"

"I don't think so. He insists he didn't. And he was still... well, you saw him. If he'd taken his clothes off, and gotten dressed again in his condition, he wouldn't look so put together still."

"Right. And he called you from her hotel?"

"Yeah. I damn near hung up on him."

Abby hugged him. "But you didn't. Because he's your brother. And you love him. And he'd come get you in the middle of the night."

"He would, and he has." Tobias sighed. "He's in love with Cassidy. I can't hold that against him."

"Our brother's in love. I never thought it'd happen."

Tobias smiled. "It was bound to happen sooner or later. At least this time, she's a keeper."

"I'm sorry it didn't work out the way you wanted it to."

Tobias shrugged. "It's hard to compete with Deacon Carmichael."

"Oh, I don't know. Tobias Carmichael is quite the catch, too."

He kissed her on the forehead. "Get some sleep."

"Is he going to be okay in there?"

"He'll be fine. He probably won't be fine when he wakes up. But for now, he's fine."

The sound of knocking woke Tobias. "Go away."

"It's Abby. Open up."

Tobias sighed, then got out of bed and went to the door. He unlocked it and opened it a crack. Abby pushed her way inside, then covered her eyes when she saw he was in his underwear.

"Gross."

"You woke me up. I don't sleep fully dressed." He picked his pants up off the floor and put them on. "Why are you banging on my door at..." He checked his watch. "Eight o'clock?"

"Deacon isn't answering his door."

"I don't blame him. He's probably hungover as hell." He yawned and scratched at his whiskered chin.

"He's not answering his phone, either. I'm worried about him."

Tobias scowled. "What do you want me to do?"

"Come knock on his door."

"Do you think he's going to answer my knock?"

"Just try. Please."

Tobias sighed again then picked his phone up off the bedside table. He dialed Deacon's number. After five rings, he ended the call. "Shit." He pulled on a t-shirt and slipped on his boots. "If he answers and cusses us out for waking him up, I'm blaming it on you, then going back to bed."

"Fine. I just want to know he's okay."

They went to Deacon's door and Tobias knocked. When they got no response, he knocked again. "Deacon. Open up."

Abby looked at him. "See?"

Tobias spotted a woman from the housekeeping staff and went to talk to her. He gave her a smiled, and she blushed.

"I was wondering if you could help me out. My brother was a bit wasted last night and now he's not answering the door. We're a little worried about him. Any chance you could open the door for us?"

She glanced at Abby, who was still at Deacon's door. "I'm sorry. I can't. It's against hotel policy."

"Are you sure?"

She nodded. "Yes. I can call security, though. They can open it for you."

"Thank you. Will you call them please?"

She nodded and headed for a wall-mounted phone down the hall.

Tobias went back to Abby. "She's calling security. So, if he's just sleeping in there, they'll probably be pissed."

"I'm sorry. I have a feeling. You know?"

"I'm here, aren't I?"

A few minutes later, a security guard appeared and walked toward them. He didn't seem all that excited about helping them.

"What seems to be the problem?"

Tobias smiled at him, which didn't have the same effect it had on the woman. "Sorry. I'm Tobias Carmichael. This is our brother's room. We've been trying to contact him and he's not answering the phone or the door."

"Do you suspect there's a problem? Does he have a health issue?"

"Not exactly. He was rather drunk last night when we left him."

The security guard looked Tobias over, then glanced at Abby. "And who are you?"

"Abby. I'm the sister. I promise you. We're not up to anything. We're just concerned."

With a sigh, the guard pulled out a key card and unlocked the door. Before he opened it, he looked at Tobias again. "We're not going to catch him in a compromising position, are we?"

"No, sir. He wasn't in any condition to... No. He's alone."

The guard opened the door a few inches. "What's his name?"

"Deacon Carmichael."

"Mr. Carmichael, this is hotel security. Are you okay?"

When there was no answer, he opened the door wider. Tobias pushed by him and entered the room. The bed was empty. Tobias went to the bathroom and checked inside, then turned to Abby.

"Well, shit. Where the hell is he?" He looked at the security guard. "Sorry. It seems our brother slipped out."

"It does seem that way, doesn't it?"

Abby looked around. "His things are gone."

Tobias scanned the room. "Dammit."

The guard looked at them both. "Are we good here?"

Tobias nodded. "Yeah. Thanks." He sat on the bed as the guard left, then looked at Abby. "Where the hell is he?"

"Breakfast?"

"With all of his stuff? Besides, I doubt he'd be able to hold anything down this morning."

Abby sat next to Tobias. "Oh, Deacon. What have you done?" She turned toward Tobias. "Maybe he went to see Cassidy. To profess his love."

Tobias stood. "That's not what he did. He's gone."

"What do you mean, gone? He can't be gone. He'd never just take off."

Tobias looked at her and held out his arms. "The man is gone." He headed for the door. "Pack your stuff. I'm going to go talk to the front desk."

Abby nodded as Tobias left the room. He returned to his room and got his cell phone. He knew it'd be fruitless, but he dialed Deacon's phone. When he got no response, he headed downstairs.

The front desk confirmed Deacon checked out of his room and paid the bill. He'd then asked about the nearest rental car service. Tobias headed for the elevator and was so distracted he ran into someone.

"Oh. Sorry." He was surprised to see it was Skyler. "Oh, it's you."

"Good morning. You look as out of it as Deacon did."

Tobias took his arm. "When did you see Deacon?"

"About an hour ago."

"Where?"

Skyler shrugged. "Right here. He looked pretty hungover."

"I'm sure he did. What did he say?"

"Nothing. Just good morning, and that he was headed out. What's going on?"

Tobias shook his head. "Nothing."

"Come on. Deacon hungover? You are obviously concerned about him. What happened?"

Tobias took Skyler's arm and led him to a corner. "Deacon and I were...having a thing. But we're okay now."

"Okay. So what's the problem?"

"He's gone AWOL."

"Deacon?"

"Yeah. I know. Sounds impossible. But it's true."

"Where is he?"

Tobias cocked his head. "I don't know. That's what AWOL means."

"Right. But it's Deacon. Mr. Dependable. Mr. Always Do The Right Thing."

"Well, everyone has a breaking point, I guess. I'm sure it's temporary. But in the meantime, I need to find him."

"What can I do?"

Tobias patted his shoulder. "Thanks, but nothing. Except keep this to yourself."

"Of course."

Tobias nodded and started to walk away, then stopped and turned back. "And tell your dad the Carmichaels are interested in Scott Bonner's stallion. Tell him we'll pay top dollar to get him."

Skyler grinned. "That's my inheritance you're messing with."

Tobias shrugged. "I'm pretty sure there will still be plenty left over for you."

Tobias and Abby left Abilene an hour later with a Mexican saddle and the Arabian gelding. Once they got to the outskirts of town, Abby glanced at Tobias.

"So, how much did we pay for my new horse?"

Tobias shook his head. "Don't ask."

Abby laughed. "I hope he's worth it."

"You better ride the hell out of him."

They were both quiet for a while before Abby spoke again. "Where do you think he went?"

"I'm sure he just wanted to clear his head a little. He'll be back."

"So, we're going to go home and wait for him to show up?"

"Hell no. I'm going to go find him."

"Can I come with you?"

"No. You need to stay with Mother. She's not going to understand why Deacon didn't come back with us."

"What are we going to tell her?"

"I don't know. I'll think of something."

Chapter Twenty-Three

"Start making sense, Tobias."

C assidy was in the barn feeding the horses their evening meal when she heard someone behind her. She turned, hoping it was Deacon. It wasn't.

"Tobias?"

"Hi." He walked over to her.

"What are you doing here? Is everything okay?"

"Um...No. Not really."

She tossed the alfalfa she was holding, then brushed off her hands and looked at him. Something was definitely up.

"What's going on?"

"Well, first off, I want to apologize for the other day. I should've stayed and talked it out with you."

"It's alright. Are you and Deacon okay?"

"Yeah. I think we are."

"Then why are you here? And where's Deacon?"

"So, you haven't heard from him today?"

"I haven't heard from him since Friday. I was hoping he'd call me over the weekend. But he didn't. And I didn't know if I should call him."

Tobias took a deep breath. "Oh boy. Okay. Idiot."

"Tobias. Just tell me what the hell is going on."

"Right. Sorry." He cleared his throat and took off his hat. "Deacon is gone."

The word gone, for some reason, didn't make sense to her. "What do you mean, gone?"

"He took off this morning. And I don't know where he is. He won't answer the phone."

Cassidy took her phone from her pocket and dialed Deacon's number. After six rings, she ended the call, stashed her phone, and sat down. Suddenly gone made perfect sense.

"Tell me everything."

"Okay. Um...Friday and Saturday, I was an ass. As you can imagine. Saturday was the benefit dinner and silent auction. We overpaid for a Mexican saddle Abby wanted. Then we really overpaid for an Arabian we have no need for. That was my doing."

"I'm trying to be patient here, Tobias."

"Right. Saturday night Deacon went to the mixer by himself, because I wouldn't go with him. He hates those things and likes to have me there, so we can joke around and talk about people. It makes the time go by faster. Anyway, he went alone and somehow ended up drinking. A lot. He was...smashed."

Something else that didn't make sense to her. "Deacon got drunk?"

"Really, really drunk. And he ran into Rachel."

"Who's Rachel?"

"Rachel broke his heart about eleven years ago. He thought she loved him. But it turned out she loved the Carmichael name, and all that came with it."

She recalled their conversation at the gala about women only being interested in his money. "So why would he want to spend time with her?"

"Because he was drunk." Tobias sat on a bale of hay and dropped his hat next to him. "He ended up going to her hotel across town."

Cassidy got to her feet. "He did what?"

Tobias stood, too. "He didn't do anything with her. I'm sure he was surprised to find himself there." He looked at her for a moment. "I promise you, he didn't do anything with Rachel. He never made it to her room."

Not totally convinced, Cassidy sat back down. "Please go on."

"He called me. It was two in the morning. He had no idea where he was or how to get back to our hotel." Tobias sat again, too. "I figured out where he was and I went to pick him up. I had to know, so I asked him point-blank if he was in love with you."

"And?"

"He said you were the one." He took a deep breath, then nodded. "He loves you, Cassidy. I can't stand in the way of that. Or be mad at him for it."

She took a moment. It was definitely welcome news. "But he was extremely drunk when he said it."

"That's how I know he meant it. No walls, no worrying about hurting my feelings. It was an uninhibited, honest answer."

Cassidy felt her eyes grow moist. "So, how did you get from there to him being gone?"

"When we got up this morning, he wasn't in his room. He checked out and rented a car."

She stood. "Where would he go?"

Tobias shrugged. "Believe me, I've thought about nothing else. I haven't figured it out yet. But I will." He got to his feet and went to her. "I'm sorry. This is so un-Deaconlike, I didn't see it coming."

She hugged him and started to cry. Tobias backed away. "Don't cry. I can't take a woman crying."

She wiped her eyes and sniffed. "Sorry."

"No. It's not you. It's me. It's just a thing I have."

She wiped her eyes again. "So, how do we find him?"

"I know if I think about it hard enough. It'll come to me. Probably in the middle of the night."

"And you'll go bring him back?"

"Of course. But this is Deacon we're talking about. The man hasn't taken a day off in ten years. He can't walk away. It's not in his nature. Even if I don't figure out where he is. He'll be back."

Cassidy sighed. "If you don't want to see me cry, then you might want to leave. Because I'm not going to be able to hold it in much longer."

Tobias took a step toward her. "What the hell." He put his arms around her and Cassidy melted into him as she let herself go. He rubbed her back. "I know. I know."

When Tobias pulled in front of the house, Abby came off the porch and met him at the truck door. "Has she heard from him?"

"No."

"Have you figured out where he'd go?"

"No."

Tobias stepped around her and went onto the porch. Abby followed him. "So, what are you going to do?"

"I'm going to go have a drink. Then I'll think some more."

As he opened the door, Ruthie stepped out and closed it behind her. She took Tobias' arm.

"Just what's going on, young man? Where's Deacon?"

Tobias backed away from her. When Ruthie was angry, she was intimidating. "I don't know. But I'm working on finding him."

Ruthie put her hands on her hips. "Why would he do this? What happened in Abilene?"

"Nothing happened in Abilene. It happened long before that."

She pointed at him. "Start making sense, Tobias."

"I'm trying." He took a breath. "It's Cassidy. He's got this notion that he's betraying me."

"That's ridiculous." She studied him for a moment. "Did you make him feel that way?"

"Not on purpose. I liked her too. I liked her first. But no."

"So his damn sense of honor is behind this?"

"Yeah. I think so. I can't think of any other reason he'd take off."

"You need to go find him."

"I know. That's what I'm trying to do."

Ruthie hugged him. "Thank you." She turned and went into the house, and Tobias looked at Abby.

"What was that?"

Abby smiled. "That was Ruthie."

Tobias started for the door again, but stopped when a car drove up and parked behind his truck. The man who got out was Phil Tillman, the family lawyer.

Tobias shook his head. "Shit."

Phil came onto the porch. "Tobias."

"Phil."

"I've been trying to get a hold of Deacon. Is he home?"

Tobias glanced at Abby. "He's out. Can I help you?"

"Out? What do you mean out? He's not answering his phone."

He really didn't have the patience to deal with Phil right now. "We've been in Abilene all weekend. I'm not sure where he is. But he'll be back soon."

Phil held up a file. "Can I leave this with you? I need his signature on quite a few things."

"Sure." Tobias took the folder from him. "I'll see that he gets it." *As soon as he gets his ass back home.*

"Thank you. And have him call me."

Tobias watched Phil leave, then scowled at Abby. "Deacon's gone less than ten hours and all hell's breaking loose."

Abby took the file. "I'll put this on his desk. You go get that drink. I think you've earned it."

"Thank you." He headed for the door once more. As he opened it, Tanner was on the other side. "Jeez, kid."

"Sorry. I just want to know what's going on. Where's Deacon?"

Tobias looked at Abby and she took Tanner's arm.

"Come sit down. I'll fill you in. Tobias needs to have a drink."

Tanner glanced at Tobias. "You might want to talk to Mother first. She's kind of upset."

Tobias went into the house to pour himself a shot of rum. He drank it down before he went to his mother's room and knocked on the door.

"Mother. It's Tobias." When he heard a faint response, he opened the door. Faith was sitting by the window and he went and sat next to her. She spent hours a day sitting on the window seat, staring at the meadow behind the barn.

She took his hand. "Where's Deacon? I haven't seen him since you came back."

"He stayed in Abilene. He had some business with one of the horse dealers. About a couple of horses we bought."

She looked at him and he felt she knew he was lying to her. But then she smiled. "Will you have him come see me when he gets in?"

"Of course."

"Thank you, dear." She turned away from him and looked out the window again.

Tobias stood, kissed her on the cheek, then left the room. "Who knew talking to her would be the easiest of all of them?"

He poured himself another shot, then went to the living room and sat on the couch. "Where the hell are you, Deacon?"

"I might know."

He turned as Tanner approached the couch.

"Do you want me to guess?"

"No. I think he'd go somewhere quiet. Where he could be alone and think."

"Right. That much I figured out. You know where that might be?"

"Grandpa's fishing cabin."

Tobias sat up and set his empty glass down. "Shit. You're a genius."

Tanner smiled. "I don't know about that."

"Of course, that's where he went." Tobias stood and hugged Tanner. "A friggin' genius."

"Can I come with you?"

Tobias took a step back. "No."

"Why?"

"Because this is between him and me. I'll go at first light." He patted Tanner's shoulder. "You stay here and be the man of the house. Of course, Abby might have something to say about that."

Tanner frowned. "It really sucks being the youngest sometimes."

"Yeah, maybe. But being the second oldest isn't ideal either."

"If he's up there, where did he get a horse? You can't drive past the bridge."

"We were at a horse sale and auction. All he had to do was buy or borrow one. Along with a trailer and something to haul it with." Tobias frowned. "He sure accomplished a lot in a very short period of time, while massively hungover."

Tanner smiled. "Well, we are talking about Deacon."

"Yes. We are."

"What if you ride up there and I'm wrong?"

Tobias shook his head. "You're not wrong, kid. You're a damn genius."

"So you've said."

Chapter Twenty-Four

"Superman has a hotel?"

Deacon had just cast his line when he heard a twig snap behind him. He glanced over his shoulder.

"Took you long enough."

Tobias walked up to him. "What the hell are you doing?"

"Fishing."

"I see that. Why?"

Deacon sighed. "Sometimes a man just needs to fish."

"Wow. That's prophetic."

Deacon watched his line for a moment, then reeled it in and prepared to cast it again. Tobias pointed to a spot on the far side of a rock.

"Right there. I guarantee there's a fish there."

"Do you want to put a little wager on that?"

"Sure. If there's a fish in that hole, you come back with me."

"And if there's not?"

"Then you try another hole."

"Are you hungry?"

"Yeah. I've spent the last four hours on a horse. Missed breakfast."

"I propose a different wager."

"Okay."

"If there's a fish behind that rock. I'll fry it up for dinner and we'll talk about me going home with you tomorrow morning."

"And if there's not?"

"I'll keep fishing until we have dinner and you get to clean them."

"Okay. Fish for dinner sounds good."

Deacon cast his line, and they both watched it for a few moments.

Tobias took off his hat and knelt on the shore. "Dammit. I was sure there would be one back there."

Deacon reeled in his line again, and cast to a pool a foot further beyond the rock. "That's where the fish is." A moment later, he felt a tug on the line and he set the hook.

Tobias sat and wrapped his arms around his knees. "Do you ever get tired of always being right?"

"Nope." He played the fish for a few minutes before bringing the twelve inch rainbow trout into shore. He held it up. "This will feed me. I'll have to catch another for you." He looked at Tobias. "Did you bring a bedroll? The cabin is pretty sparse."

"I have everything I need."

Deacon cast the line again to the same spot. "I'm guessing this guy had a friend." It took a third cast to the spot, but he caught another fish, and smiled at Tobias. "I'll go get a fire going while you clean these guys."

"Yeah. Thanks."

Deacon had a nice fire burning when Tobias brought the cleaned fish up from the river. He set them on a rock beside the cast-iron skillet sitting next to the fire, then frowned at the lemon and the stick of butter.

"How the hell do you have that with you?"

"You know I'm always prepared. I knew I'd be eating fish tonight."

"When did you get here?"

"Last night."

"I saw the truck and trailer. Did you borrow them, or do we have a new horse and trailer?"

"I borrowed the trailer and bought the horse for a good price. After you spent a small fortune on the Arabian, I thought I should watch what I spend."

"Funny. We can sell the Arabian."

"Not for what you paid for it."

"Probably not. At least it was for a good cause."

Deacon held the pan with the butter and lemon juice over the fire until it melted, then he put the filleted fish into it and set it on a grate over the fire. He dug into his pack and took out a can of green beans and a can of sliced boiled potatoes. He tossed the potatoes to Tobias.

"Open that and fry them in that other pan with butter."

"So, are we just going to cook dinner and pretend I didn't follow you here to the middle of nowhere after you disappeared from the hotel without saying a word to Abby or me?"

"Yes. That's exactly what we're going to do."

"Deacon."

He glanced at Tobias. "We'll talk after we eat."

"Fine. I'm holding you to it."

"I don't suppose you brought a bottle of wine with you?"

Tobias laughed. "Wine? Of course not. I did bring a bottle of scotch, though."

Deacon smiled. "Good man."

"Unless, of course, you've had enough scotch for a while."

He thought for a moment. "I can have a shot or two."

"You were really toasted the other night."

"I don't remember a lot of it. But I remember something about Superman."

"Yeah. We were at his hotel."

Deacon frowned. "Superman has a hotel?"

Tobias laughed. "According to you, he does." He looked at Deacon. "You didn't sleep with Rachel, right?"

"Hell no. I remember that, too. She really wanted me to, though."

"Yeah. That's what you keep saying."

Deacon laughed. "I did think about it for almost two seconds."

"And why didn't you go through with it?"

"You know why."

⁂

They both ate their fill and were on a second shot of scotch when Tobias leaned against his saddle and put his feet close to the fire. He glanced at Deacon, who was staring into the flames.

"Okay, big brother. Time to talk."

Deacon sighed. "I just needed to clear my head."

"You have a woman back home worried sick about you. I had to comfort her while she cried. And you know how I feel about crying women."

"She cried?"

"You ignored her all weekend, then you disappear and don't come home. Did you think she'd be happy about that? That she'd understand?" He shook his head. "She doesn't understand, man. And neither do I."

Deacon took a sip of his scotch. "I don't know how to do this. I haven't been in a relationship. Not a real relationship in eleven years."

"What you had with Rachel wasn't a relationship."

"I know that now. I was a stupid kid. I'm still stupid. I'm just not a kid anymore."

"You're not stupid." He smiled at Deacon. "Well, you're here instead of there with her, so you're a little stupid."

"How do I do this? Where do I start?"

"Being in the same town would be a good first step."

Deacon looked at him for a moment. "I hope you realize I tried like hell to fight this. I didn't want to come between you and Cassidy. I know you really liked her."

"Water under the bridge, brother. She broke up with me before you two went carnal in the classroom."

Deacon smiled. "Not my finest moment."

"I don't think she was complaining. The bottom line is. You want her. And she wants you. So why the hell are you here drinking scotch with me?"

"That's a damn good question."

"Leave at first light?"

"Hell yeah."

***

The cabin was old and musty, so they slept outside by the fire and reminisced about coming to the cabin as kids. Tobias, being seven years younger, didn't spend as much time there with their grandfather as Deacon did. And once their father died, their grandfather, like their mother, was never quite the same. He died of a heart attack two years after he lost his son.

But there were plenty of good times to remember and it was a place just the two of them shared. Tobias brought Tanner there once two years ago, and Abby had never been. Without the memories of their father and grandfather, it wasn't the same for the two younger Carmichaels.

When Deacon fell quiet, Tobias knew his brother had gone to sleep. He sat and put another piece of wood on the fire before settling down for the night. He was more disappointed than sad about Cassidy. He'd felt from the beginning she wasn't nearly as interested in him as he was in her. He'd just hoped he'd win her over at some point. But it wasn't meant to be. Cassidy and Deacon were destined to be together. He could see that now. And he accepted it. He just hoped someday he'd find someone who would set off the fireworks. Preferably for both of them.

***

"Come on. We're burning daylight." Tobias looked up at Deacon standing over him. When Deacon started to nudge him again with his foot, Tobias pointed at him. "Don't nudge me again. Or I'll knock you on your ass."

Deacon laughed. "Then get the hell out of bed."

Tobias looked at the hard ground he was lying on. "Not much of a bed. How did our ancestors do this for weeks or months at a time?"

"They were real men."

Tobias sat up with a grunt. His leg hurt from the long ride yesterday and the even longer night on the ground. He held his hand out to Deacon. "Give this modern, and not so real man a hand up, will ya?"

Deacon took his hand and pulled Tobias to his feet. "Are you okay?"

"I just need to walk off the stiffness." He headed for a stand of trees. "And while I do that, I'll get rid of the scotch in my bladder."

"Hurry up. I want to go."

Tobias limped toward the trees. "Now you're in a damn hurry."

When he returned to the camp, Deacon had saddled both horses and put dirt over the firepit.

Tobias looked at him. "So, no breakfast?"

Deacon opened his saddle bag and tossed Tobias a granola bar. "We'll get something when we're on the road."

"Somehow, I don't see that happening. Once we're on the road, you're not going to want to stop for anything."

"I promise we'll get something to eat."

"I'm going to hold you to that."

"Besides, we need to drop the truck and trailer off in Evanston."

"You already made arrangements to leave them?"

"Of course."

"Oh, right. I forgot. You're Deacon Carmichael. Even when it seems you've taken off without a plan. You always have a plan."

"I've never been spontaneous, Tobias. You know that."

"Yeah. I know. Although I'm pretty sure your moment in the classroom was spontaneous. Even you couldn't have planned that."

"Okay. So once in my life I was spontaneous."

Tobias patted his shoulder. "You should really try it more often. You never know where it might lead."

Deacon grinned. "It did feel pretty damn good."

They made the four-hour trip in three and a half, and by the time they got to the two trucks and horse trailers, Tobias was in quite a bit of pain. Deacon insisted Tobias sit in the truck while he loaded the horses into the trailer Tobias had brought.

When he was done, he went to Tobias.

"Are you okay to drive?"

"Yeah. No problem."

"You just need to make it to Evanston, then I'll take over."

"And that's what? Ten miles?"

"Yeah. You good?"

Tobias gave him a thumbs up, then closed the door of the truck. "I'll follow you."

They drove to the fairgrounds outside of Evanston and Deacon parked the truck and empty horse trailer in the lot. He then went inside to drop off the keys.

While he did that, Tobias got out and walked around for a few minutes. The pain in his leg was always there, but most of the time it was manageable and he could deal with it. But sometimes, when he overdid, such as chasing the hounds on Gala weekend, or spending hours in the saddle, it wasn't manageable. He'd be glad to get home and lose himself for a while in a bottle of rum.

When Deacon came out of the office, Tobias got into the passenger seat.

"Take us home, brother. Actually, take us somewhere to eat. That granola bar has long since done its job."

"Um... I'll stop at the gas station and you can get whatever you want."

Tobias turned in his seat. "You promised we'd eat."

"And we will. Just not at a restaurant."

"You suck, man."

"I know. But I've got to get back." He pulled into a gas station with a mini market. "I suppose you want me to go in."

Tobias raised an eyebrow for his answer.

"Right. I'll load up. Do you want to pump the gas?" When Tobias didn't answer, or make a move to get out of the truck, Deacon nodded. "I'll pump the gas." He opened his door.

Tobias looked at him. "Get me a fifth of rum to go along with my *breakfast*."

"Coming right up."

Chapter Twenty-Five

"I'm going to shoot my brother."

C assidy took a long trail ride to get her mind off of Deacon. She didn't understand why he took off. It was so out of character. And now it'd been two days since she heard from Tobias. She wanted to call Abby and see if she knew anything, but decided not to. If Deacon was back, someone would let her know.

When she got close enough to the ranch to see the barn, she saw a white Jeep with a horse trailer, parked in front of it. There was only one person she knew who drove a white Cherokee. She nudged Stanley into a lope until she got close, then she slowed down when she saw Deacon standing next to the vehicle.

When she got closer, he walked toward her and took Stanley's bridle.

"Deacon."

"Hi."

Cassidy dismounted, and he took the reins from her. "You're back."

"Yes. I am. And I owe you an apology."

She shook her head. "I don't need an apology. I just need you to tell me you're back for good."

"I'm back for good. I'm done being stupid. I'm—"

Cassidy stepped up to him and kissed him, then whispered into his ear. "Don't ever do that to me again."

He hugged her and kissed her neck. "I'll never leave you again."

She leaned back a few inches and looked at him. "I should be really mad at you."

"I know."

"Are you and Tobias okay?"

"Yeah. We're good." He leaned in and kissed her again.

She took a step back. "My grandfather is gone for a couple of days. Can I cook you dinner?"

He smiled. "I'd like that."

"Help me put Stanley away."

"Hold on. I brought you something. An, 'I'm sorry for being an idiot' gift. Stay right there." He went to the back of the trailer and she heard what sounded a lot like he was unloading a horse. He came around the trailer leading the horse he'd bought out from under her grandfather.

"Deacon."

"I believe this horse belongs to you."

"You can't give me a horse."

"Of course I can." He handed her the reins. "See. I just did."

"I'll take him for now, but we're going to talk about this further."

"Fine. Just not tonight."

They unsaddled Stanley and put him in his stall. While Cassidy was feeding him, Deacon put the new horse in another stall, then went to check on Precious. Even though it hadn't been that long since he was born, the colt was noticeably bigger. Cassidy came up beside Deacon and he glanced at her.

"He's getting big."

"But he's still Precious. Look at that face."

"Pretty damn cute."

She went to the new horse. "You really shouldn't have."

"He looks pretty good in here."

She rubbed the horse's nose. "Does he have a name, yet?"

"No. Well, he came with a name. But it's a stupid one. And he doesn't respond to it. So you can name him anything you want."

She studied the horse for a moment, then glanced at Deacon. "What's your middle name?"

"Franklin."

"Perfect. I'll name him Franklin."

"Really?"

"Yes. It's perfect."

Cassidy took Deacon's hand, and they left the barn and headed for the house. "So, where did you go?"

"I went to my grandfather's fishing cabin. Four hours by horse. Great fishing, though. Tobias showed up yesterday afternoon."

"You own the property?"

"It was the first section of land the family bought. It's separated from the ranch by a strip of forest service land. You can get to it from the east side of the ranch, but it takes twice as long."

"Did you fish? Or just sulk?"

Deacon laughed. "I didn't go there to sulk. I went there to think."

She glanced at him. "You couldn't think here?"

"Not with you this close to me."

She didn't want to let him off too easily. But it was really good to see him. She tried to stay strong. "What did you need to think about?"

"How the hell I was going to pull this off."

"Pull what off?" How did she forget in just a few days how intense his eyes were. The way he looked at her with such... Was it longing?

He stopped walking and took her hands in his. "I want to be the man you deserve, Cassidy. I'm not sure I'm quite there yet."

"Well, in my mind, I'm trying to figure out how to be the woman *you* deserve."

He grinned. "I guess we just need to figure this out together."

"Sounds like a good plan." They started walking again. "How hungry are you?"

"Starving. I had a granola bar this morning at about seven o'clock."

"That's all?"

"Yeah. I promised Tobias we'd eat when we got to the highway, but I couldn't take the time. I had to get back to you."

"I bet that made Tobias a bit unhappy."

"When we stopped for gas, I loaded him up with junk food. He survived. Of course, the rum helped."

"Rum?"

"Four hours in. Four hours back out, and a long night sleeping on the ground. He needed a little medicinal help."

"So you didn't eat any of his snacks?"

"He wouldn't give me any. He was punishing me."

Cassidy laughed. "Well, you kind of deserved it."

"I suppose."

They went into the house and Deacon followed Cassidy to the kitchen. She waved toward the table. "You don't mind eating in the kitchen, do you?"

"I don't care where I eat as long as you're sitting across the table from me."

He just kept saying the right thing. "What did you and Tobias eat last night? Something out of a can?"

"Trout. The beans and potatoes were out of a can, though."

She opened the refrigerator. "How do you feel about lasagna?"

"Love it."

She took out a glass pan and set it on the counter. "I made this for Grandpa and me, but he had to leave, so it's all ready. I just need to warm it up."

She turned on the oven. "Do you want a drink or anything while we wait? It'll take about thirty minutes."

"I'm good. Thanks."

"Okay. I'm going to go wash the horse off of me. I'll be back in a few minutes."

"I'll be here."

Cassidy went into her room. He was here. He was actually here, having dinner with her. Did she dare hope things would be okay now? Was Deacon really done trying to run from his feelings? She hoped so. Because seeing him again and kissing him again, confirmed how she felt. She was in love with Deacon Carmichael.

She took a quick shower and changed her clothes. She didn't know where the night was going to end. But she hoped... She looked around her room. It was a bit of a mess. She did a quick sweep through the room, then straightened out the bed. She sighed. Maybe it was too soon. But maybe it wasn't. She would know when and if the opportunity presented itself.

When she left her room, she found Deacon in the living room, looking at the pictures on the mantle.

He glanced over his shoulder at her. "I remember you like this. Pink cowboy hat, just like I said. Riding Bumble Bee."

She came up beside him. "I still can't believe you remember my horse's name."

"How old were you there?"

She looked at the picture for a moment. "Ten. I think. Maybe eleven."

"Which means I was in high school. And soon to be leaving for Yale."

"Eight years difference in age back then was a lot different from eight years now."

"Thank God." He picked up a baby picture of her. "Talk about precious."

"I was pretty cute."

He set the picture down and put his arms around her. "You still are. Actually, more like beautiful." He kissed her, then took a step back. "Should be about time for lasagna."

He seemed to be trying to control himself. Not moving too fast, too soon. She appreciated it. But it was slightly frustrating as well. "Let's go check."

Deacon watched Cassidy take the lasagna from the oven and set it in the middle of the table. Then she handed him a plate, a napkin, and silverware.

"Something to drink?"

"Do you have a beer?"

She went to the refrigerator and took out two beers, then sat across the table from him.

She put her napkin in her lap and picked up her fork. "This is a little weird."

"How so?"

She smiled. "You've been so out of reach since I met you. I can't quite believe you're actually here."

"I have been a bit of an ass."

"No. You just thought you knew what you wanted. What you felt you needed to do."

He held up his beer. "To getting my head out of my ass."

She tapped his bottle with hers. "Welcome to the light."

He took a bite of the lasagna, then nodded. "Mmm. Very good." He took a sip of beer. "What else can you cook?" He figured as long as he kept talking, he'd be able to control his urge to pick her up and carry her off to the bedroom. It's all he had thought about since yesterday afternoon.

"I'm not an experienced cook, by any means. But I have a few things I cook well."

"Well, this is fantastic." It truly was and he was impressed.

"It probably doesn't hurt that you're starving."

"Even if I wasn't starving. This is damn good."

"You enjoy. And eat until you're full. Then we're going to go into the living room, and you're going to tell me all about your adventures Saturday night."

"My adventures?" He shook his head. "Damn Tobias."

"He gave me an abridged version. I'd like to hear the whole story."

"It's a little foggy, but I'll do my best." He wondered just what Tobias had said to her.

Deacon had a second serving, then offered to help Cassidy with the dishes. But she sent him into the living room to get a fire going in the fireplace. By the time she joined him, he was on the couch and the fire was burning nicely.

Cassidy sat next to him and he put his arm around her. "Thank you for dinner."

"Thank you for being here to eat it." She put a hand on his leg. "So, tell me about Rachel."

He laughed. "Wow. Okay. Not much to tell. I met her right after I got home from college. I thought she was someone she wasn't. She wanted to be Mrs. Carmichael. I just happened to be the one she could get close to."

"I'm sorry."

"A lesson learned."

"So, tell me about Rachel on Saturday night."

"I'm going to shoot my brother." He took a breath. "I was at the bar having one last drink. I'd already had too many. But that was the only way to get through the evening without Tobias there to keep me entertained. She showed up. I bought her a drink. And a few rounds later, I found myself in a cab headed to her hotel."

"So, you were really drunk at this point?"

"Yes. One minute I was in the bar and the next I was in the cab. Then a few minutes after that, I was in the elevator."

Cassidy looked at him. "You got in the elevator with her?"

"Yes. And she kissed me. And then whispered something obscene in my ear, and suddenly I knew I was in the wrong place with the wrong woman."

"You didn't go into her room?"

"No. I didn't get out of the elevator. Until I went to the lobby, that is. I went outside and realized I had no idea where I was or how to get back to my hotel."

"So you called Tobias?"

"Yep. Even though he was still mad at me. I knew he'd come. God knows I've dragged his drunk ass home plenty of times."

"And why did you leave the next morning?"

He looked at her for a moment. He wanted to be honest with her. "At that point, I still felt like I could fix things. But about two hours into the horse ride, I realized I didn't want to fix it. I wanted...you."

"You could've turned around and come back out."

"I also wanted to fish." She squeezed his knee, and he laughed. "I needed to take some time to wrap my head around the whole having a relationship thing."

"And how'd that go?"

He turned and looked at her. "I'm here with you. And I'm going to do my best to do right by you. Because I'm falling for you. I'm falling hard."

She put her hand on his face. "I'm going to tell you something I hope won't scare you, but I feel I need to let you know."

"Okay."

"I already fell."

That was pretty much the best three words he'd ever heard. "You did? When?"

"About a minute after I called you an asshole at the gala."

He nodded. "It was well deserved. And honestly, if you want to know the truth. I fell for you at the gala, too."

"When?"

"Right after you inferred I was an elitist snob."

Cassidy smiled. "Okay. I wasn't on my best behavior that night."

"But you were right on both accounts. I was in full Deacon Carmichael mode."

She shook her head. "I don't think that's the real Deacon Carmichael." She kissed him. "I think I'm sitting with the real you."

"So, I have a question."

"What's that?"

"Is bacon and eggs one of the things you cook well?"

"No." She smiled. "But I make one hell of a Denver omelet."

"Really? I happen to love Denver omelets."

Cassidy stood and took Deacon's hand. "I want to show you something."

He got to his feet and let her lead him down the hallway. She stopped at a door.

"This is my bedroom."

He peered in the door. "Very nice. Thanks for showing it to me." He started to walk away, and she took his arm.

"Deacon, where do you think you're going?"

He turned back with a smile and put his arms around her. "Are you sure you want an elitist asshole sharing your bed?"

"Well, you do own the second biggest ranch in Texas."

He put a hand to his chest. "Oh. Ouch."

Cassidy laughed. "Too soon?"

"It will always be too soon for that."

She hugged him. "You have nothing to worry about. I'm set to inherit the...thirtieth or so largest ranch in Texas, so I have no need for your money."

"What a relief." He picked her up and carried her into the room. "Honestly, at this point, I couldn't care less if you were after my money. I'd give it all to you. Every damn cent." He put her down and laid next to her.

"Well, fortunately, all I want is you."

Does Tobias find his fireworks person? Tobias
https://www.amazon.com/dp/B0C5GGL25B

More Books By Leigh Fenty

The Three Oaks Ranch Series

Memories Of You

The Good Son

The Wayward Son

Little Sis

The Carmichael Series

Deacon

Tobias

Abigale

Tanner
The Christmas Wedding
Faith's Journal

The Gracie Island Series
The Deputy
The Best Woman
The Chief
The Family Man
The Visitor

Love Notes
The Last Will And Testament Of Atticus Wainwright III

The Out of Focus Series
Out Of Focus
Out Of Luck
Out Of The Deep
Out Of Time

The John O'Leary Series
The Boy In The Yellow Wellies
The Man Without A Heart

Touch
A Change Of Plans

About the Author

L eigh spends her days with cute, sexy guys. Unfortunately, they're on paper. But still, not a bad way to spend your day. She also writes about strong, independent women, who can hold their own against these irresistible guys. She's not a pure romance writer, because she breaks the rules a bit. But that's the fun part. Leigh's stories have adventure, family relationships, and the struggles life throws at you sometimes. But boy always meets girl. They tussle a bit while they figure out what they really want. Then find their happily ever after. Even if it's not what they thought it was going to be.

Printed in Great Britain
by Amazon